DARKNESS

An anthology of Dark
and Twisted Tales from

THE SONS OF TWISTED FATE

CM ANGUS
GARETH CLEGG
NICK STEAD
OWEN TOWNEND
IAN F WHITE
TIM TAYLOR
AQIB ALI

TWISTED FATE
PUBLISHING

INTRODUCTION

With much of the world in isolation, support for mental health is more important than ever. Realising this, a number of established like-minded authors formed The Sons of Twisted Fate to turn their skills to creating this collection of short stories to support the mental health charity: Mind.

The collection that you now hold is the result of a unique collaboration by a diverse group of authors, all writers of Speculative fiction (Sci-Fi, Horror and Fantasy) but all very different from one another. Each was challenged to contribute one or more short stories around the theme of Darkness.

We're very grateful for each contribution and hope you enjoy reading this collection as much as we've enjoyed putting it together.

We are also indebted to the fantastically talented, award-winning artist: Richard Rowan who kindly provided art for our cover.

Enjoy and stay safe.

The Twisted Fate Publishing team - October 2020

CONTENTS

WHO ARE THE SONS OF TWISTED FATE?

Seven silhouettes rose up into the world of man. Seven writers, hand-picked by Fate itself. Their mission: to record the stories of the strange and the unnatural, and to share them with the people of Earth.

Each has his own tales to tell. Tales of a speculative nature, designed to fascinate and excite, to intrigue and entertain, and sometimes, to chill the blood and quicken the heart.

These are the words of the Sons of Twisted Fate...

THE FADE

"A YOUNG GIRL SEARCHES FOR FORBIDDEN
LIGHT IN A FANTASY WORLD OF ETERNAL
DARKNESS."

GARETH CLEGG

In a time long forgotten, when the world was new, we angered the gods. In our foolish pride, we sought to make them follow our bidding, no longer accepting them as our saviours, but as equals we thought to surpass.

Their retribution was both total and merciless, the surface of our world destroyed by an unholy flame that consumed everything in its path. In the aeons since, we have learned our place is in the darkness, but still, some of us dare to tread where none should go, seeking the location where the light meets the dark. A place known as the Fade.

The Prophecies of Zael
The Book of Dwindling Light.

The brightness burned through the Fade, blinding Ella as she stared into its receding glow. She blinked, rubbing the heels of dirty palms into her eyes. Spots of colour floated like cave moss. When she opened them again, they had gone – just the dull grey of the Fade remained. Grey rocks in grey passageways filled the tunnel, slinking away from her into the distance. Her last torch spluttered, threatening to leave her in darkness. The bright green glow from the end of the metal stick burst back into life as she thrashed it against a rock with a clang. "What was that, Tink?"

The small animal beside her whined, rotating his neck to peer up into her pale features. Reflected in those huge shiny eyes, her dirt-encrusted face stared back, framed by scruffy braided hair, hacked into a short boyish cut at the sides. With the glowstick's light, it almost looked green, and Ella marvelled at the thought of being a pure Tone. But that was a fantasy. She was nothing, not even a glimpse of undertone in her scrawny frame.

"Did you see it?" she continued, waiting for Tink to respond.

"*Tink,*" the tiny creature replied, his skin rippling as metal plates glided over each other while he shuffled back.

"Well, I did!" Ella said, in her best attempt at a grown-up pout. She'd copied it from her sisters. They were always doing it, ending up getting what they wanted most of the time. "Come on, let's follow it."

The creature stopped, head shifting from side to side. "*Tink?*"

"Yes, and you'll keep up if you don't want to get lost here. All alone. In the dark."

She strode forward, holding the glowstick high. As the circle of green light edged past her pet, he shrieked. "*Tink, Tink, Tink.*" His body segments squeaked into motion as he struggled to stay within the fading glow.

Ella stopped, turning to admonish him. "You see? You always follow in the end. No use pretending to be stubborn, is there?"

Tink leapt onto her boot, shivering as his carapace scraped against the metal buckles. "*Tink, Tink, Tink,*" he continued with a trill in his metallic voice.

She bent to lift him from the ground, moisture welling in the corner of her eye. "I'm sorry, Tink. I didn't mean to scare you. Come on, you ride up here, and we'll hunt down that light." She placed the quivering creature on her shoulder, and he nuzzled into her, segmented limbs gripping the rough cloth around her neck.

* * *

Two hours of searching the deeper areas of the Fade and Ella guessed she was as far from the settlement as she'd ever been. The hunters told tales of the Gyre, and from her recollections, she thought they must be close now.

The skittering of metal on stone announced Tink's approach. Once he'd realised she wouldn't leave him behind, he returned to travelling under his own propulsion. He preferred his independence, though wasn't averse to hitching a ride when scared. Ella chuckled. Tink couldn't really get scared. He was a construct—a clever design for sure, but still a machine—built by her father to keep his lonely girl company.

So where was the Gyre? As if in response, her belly growled, reminding her she should eat something. Rummaging through her pack, she pulled out the crumbled remains of the cracker she'd had for lunch, small fragments of dried fruit clinging to the dusty remnants of the crunchy biscuit. It didn't look at all appetising, but it was all she had left. She tilted her head back, pouring the debris into her mouth. What little moisture she had disappeared into a substance more like glue than food as she struggled to chew the thickening mass. She almost spat the sticky lump out but forced herself to swallow. At least when it hit her stomach, it might stop the rumbling.

Casting her mind back to her location, Ella reviewed her route. She'd followed the downward tunnels, passed through the Chamber of Weeping Stone and taken the leftmost path. From there, she'd squashed herself flat to crawl through the Vice, removing her precious satchel and dragging it along behind to fit through. It had only required ten minutes, but twice it tried to grab her. Her chest still ached from where her heart had thundered as she fought to contain the terror of being trapped. But, after calming herself, it was a simple matter of adjusting the belongings on her belt and unhitching where her tunic had caught in the angular rocky protrusions.

Light, what would she have done if she'd got herself wedged in tight?

She shook the shiver from her shoulders and turned her thoughts back to her mental map as Tink scraped his way across the rough floor into the circle of green from her second glowstick.

She smiled down at the tiny creature and dropped onto a smooth rock which looked a comfortable height for sitting. "Found anything?"

Tink's enormous eyes flicked up to meet hers, then lowered again. "*Tink.*"

She sighed, a thin stream of pale air condensing in the cold before her. "Thought as much. Well, looks like it's down to me again to find our way. Kyren mentioned the Weeping Stones, bearing left through the Vice and then..."

She looked down at her pet. "Why am I even telling you all this? You were there too. Why don't you lead for a while?"

"Tink, Tink," he replied, and to Ella's surprise, headed to the edge of the green-lit area, back in the direction they had come.

"We're not going home, Tink," she said as he scuttled off. "That's the wrong way."

The sound of metal on stone continued for a few seconds before changing into the grating of metal on metal, almost like someone sharpening a blade or cutting with scissors.

"What are you doing?" she called out into the darkness.

She was just about to call again when she noticed the soft green glow. Rising from her rocky chair, she held the glowstick high and moved toward the light, which was now spreading to the size of a fist and brightening. The inky silhouette of her metallic pet was thrashing his front legs before him as luminescent flecks of green splattered in drops on the surrounding rocks.

"What in the light?" Ella thrust her hand out before her,

blocking the growing brightness, which was becoming painful. She reached to her neck, pulling her goggles up to cover her watering eyes. The intense glare dimmed, and she lowered her palm. As she approached the glow, it revealed the edge of a large patch of moss. "Tink, you beauty. You found the way – follow the moss – you *were* listening!" She grasped the eight-legged creature in both hands, hugging him into her chest.

"Tink!"

She pulled back, staring down her nose at the beast as he gesticulated with glowing front legs. Had he just admonished her? She wasn't sure but left it for now. "Well done."

Ella walked over to the moss and grabbed a handful, crushing it against the rock, then followed its path around the edge of the dark grin that was the Vice.

The mossy liquid was the same they used in the glowsticks, but much brighter here, straight from the living plant. She remembered playing with her sisters and chewing the stuff. They'd all laughed at her until she'd opened her mouth, painting them with green light like a blazing torch. Then they'd scattered into the darkness to hide while she ran about trying to catch them in the beam. Ella smiled – one of the few happy memories of family life before her father died.

* * *

The darklight lenses protected her sight as Ella followed the glowing moss, but made finding safe footing much more difficult. She slowed her pace, placing her feet with great care. A slip here could prove fatal. If not killed by the fall, she'd suffer in agony, broken and bleeding until someone found her – if anyone ever did. A shiver ran down her spine. Tink clunked along just behind her, picking his way through the rough stone cavern and fields of glowmoss.

She paused, rubbing around the edge of her goggles, the metal biting at her skin as her breath plumed before her. The air grew colder as she continued downward into the heart of the Fade. Ella had never seen ice but recognised it from the stories Kyren told the children from his journeys scouting and mapping their land.

Hard water is how he'd described it to them, but most of the kids didn't understand how that might look. Myriad pinpricks of green twinkled from a rock ahead, like staring at the roof of one of the glowcaves where the worms spun silk from the vaulted ceilings. Here those glows were within arm's reach. She just needed to lean out and –

"Tink, Tink, Tink!"

Ella's arm shot back, shocked at the volume of the warning. She twisted to scowl at her pet for almost scaring her to death, but her right boot caught on something, and she lurched, her weight pulling her towards the rocky edge they'd been traversing. She thrust out an arm, trying to stop herself before she overbalanced, and hot ripping pain raged up from her palm. Her hand slid across the blood-slicked rock, the beautiful sparkling surface now dripping red into the glowmoss as she toppled out into open space. Tink squealed. The air rushed by Ella, stealing away the frantic "Tink, tink, tink!" as she plummeted into the void.

Ella slammed into a solid surface, but instead of cracking her bones into a thousand splinters, it enveloped her in its icy embrace. She gasped, gagging as liquid flooded into her throat, spluttering and gasping for breath. The crushing pressure around her body grew until her ribs felt like they were about to crack. Thrashing in the nothingness, her movements appeared unconnected to any conscious thoughts. She knew she was drowning but was powerless to resist the water's vice-like grip. Down and down she went, until spots of light danced before her eyes and her head throbbed, blood pumping a rhythmic drumbeat through her entire being. *She was dying.*

She convulsed. Once, twice, and fell still. The noise in her head faded, the pain in her chest nothing but a dull memory. Her thick braided hair yanked backwards. A shock of blistering heat, then her skin was aflame.

* * *

Ella retched on all fours, acid burning her throat. The woman beside her held her up, dark hands wrapped in a tight wad of matted braids while the girl disgorged the oily liquid next to the underground lake.

She gave another couple of dry heaves, her stomach clenching while she croaked her complaint. At last, it decided there was nothing left to bring up and released her to collapse onto the freezing ground. The pressure on her hair loosened and she turned to face the stranger, looking up into the pitch darkness.

"It's all right, child. Looks like you'll live, though I confess I was worried."

"Who?" Ella coughed and winced as fire burnt again in her raw throat.

"Whoa, girl. Keep quiet and let your body recover a little. My name isn't important, but for now, just know that I dragged you out of that pool and don't intend you any harm. Rest for a time while I think about this."

The woman reached to her belt, offering a small canteen. "Water," she said. "It will help get that greasy taste from your mouth, but not too much. Try short sips and wash it around, then spit it out. The last thing you need is to swallow any more of that oily muck."

Ella drew in a ragged breath that gurgled in her throat and nodded as she reached for the container. A few sips later and the world seemed a more pleasant place. She played the liquid around her mouth, a sticky coating dissolving from her cheeks and tongue, before spitting it back into the black lake.

Ella dragged her aching body into a sitting position. "Thank you."

The hooded woman followed her every move while Ella strained to work out where she was, but it was too dark to see anything much beyond arm's reach. As she squinted, the icy touch of the metal rims bit into her skin, and she reached up to remove her goggles. The Fade bloomed into all its twilight glory as the Darklight lenses pulled free with a sucking sound.

"Make sure none of that stuff gets in your eyes," the woman said, handing her a piece of dark cloth. Ella took it and nodded her thanks, then dabbed around her face, removing the oily residue.

"What is it?" Ella asked.

"Darkmatter—concentrated shadow."

Ella squinted back to the woman and wondered at the strange belted tunic and multiple straps running across her leather leggings. But her heart almost stopped when she noticed the woman's features, or lack of them. Her face was a hollow of darkness within the hood, and she looked no clearer now than before Ella had removed her Darklight lenses. The woman's skin seemed a mask of shadow, like the stuff in the lake beside them.

Ella sucked in a sharp breath, the icy cold raking her raw throat, and scuttled back, ignoring the pins and needles where her flesh contacted the rocky surface.

"Don't be afraid, child," the woman said, reaching forward with black palms outstretched. "I won't hurt you."

"What are you? What is this place?"

The woman pulled her hands back towards herself, leaving a smoky outline for a moment before it coalesced into her. "This is the Gyre, child. A gateway between the Shade and the Veil."

Ella felt her eyes widen and fought to stop her jaw dropping like an uneducated commoner. "And what, who are you?"

A soft chuckle came from the dark hood. "You may call me Rowen, Shadowmancer to Lady Darklight."

Ella coughed out a laugh. "Do you think I was born yesternight? Lady Darklight is a tale for children."

"Oh, and you are more than a child then?"

"Yes," Ella replied, heat burning in her cheeks. "I am but two cycles from my naming day."

"Well," Rowen said, pausing as if in deep thought, "young lady."

Ella wasn't sure if she was being mocked, but before she had time to plan a snide reply, Rowen stood, stepping a pace back. Her movement was beyond graceful, her body seeming to flow like dust in a gentle breeze.

"Perhaps you heard the legends? When you were younger, of course."

Ella rolled her eyes. "Everyone knows the tale of Lady Darklight."

"And of Shadowmancy?"

"No, I'm not aware of that. There were Shadowmakers who could control and mould the Shade?"

Rowen's shoulders slumped. "Oh, how dreadfully bland. I suppose they call what we do Shadowmaking or some such? What a dire evolution of what is the most beautiful of art forms."

Ella shrugged. "I only know what I was told."

"My apologies, you are right. It's not your fault how the truth has distorted through the ages. But what of these Shadowmakers? What do the legends tell of them?"

"Erm, they were much as the name suggests, able to make things from shadows: shapes and cloaks of darkness to hide under. That sort of thing."

"I see we still have little to live up to with your people." Rowen drew her black hands out before her, palms towards Ella, thumbs and forefingers touching.

"What are you doing?" Ella asked, pushing herself to her feet.

"Nothing to worry about. A simple demonstration of Shadowmancy, so you may trust what I speak of is the truth and not some children's story."

Rowen's voice changed, becoming a slow sibilant whisper on the edge of hearing. Ella strained to make out the words, but they were no language she recognised. They were more akin to the sound of the breeze passing through cracks in the rocks and reflecting from walls to echo off into the distance. As she waited, wisps of smoke rose from the lake surface and flowed to Rowen's palms. They focused in the gap between her hands, the deep grey becoming darker by the moment until it was solid black, indistinguishable from her skin. With a flourish, she flung her arms wide, and darkness erupted.

Rivers of shifting shadow leapt from the ground, winding around the rocky walls, leaving a stairway of onyx stone rising from the water's edge. Ella's hair spiked as if hit by a static charge, shivers running down her spine, then it grounded itself in the rock below her feet. She gazed up at the construction, unable to hide her awe. Glancing back to Rowen, Ella noticed the woman's hands were no longer black, but now faded to a deep grey at the fingertips.

"I don't believe…"

Rowen pointed up the massive stairwell. "I fear you are missing something?"

"What?" Ella replied, her gaze shifting to the stairs as a faint glow descended the new walkway, followed by a metallic scraping sound. "Tink?" she called, rushing to the construct.

"Tink. Tink. Tink," came the steady reply as her best friend descended, one step at a time.

Ella scooped him up, hugging the creature to her chest. "Oh, Tink. I thought I'd lost you."

"Tink?"

"What's wrong?" Ella asked as he twisted in her grasp, metal surfaces gliding over each other with a soft whisper.

A glowing arm stretched out toward her face. "Tink!"

Ella glared past the green glow into the carapace shell where black orbs stared back at her from Tink's reflective surface. Utter darkness where her eyes should have been, with a subtle hint of Tink's shape reflected in them like an image caught between two mirrors. Ella's head whirled as the infinite reflections hit her, and her breath sucked into her throat. Her body seemed to fall away from her.

Velvet arms caught her before she struck the rocky ground, lowering her into a sitting position. They dispersed, dark swirling wisps of nothingness as they twisted across the room to Rowen, playful, like pipe smoke, then faded back into the woman's hands.

"How? What?"

Rowen crossed to kneel beside her, palm resting on her shoulder. "Don't worry, child. 'The Realising' is always difficult."

A thin block appeared from nowhere in Rowen's hand. She offered it to the girl. "Sit, rest and eat this."

"What is it?" Ella asked, her body tilting away from the curious gift.

"Chocolate," the woman replied. "It's both sweet and bitter at the same time. You'll love it."

"How do you know?"

"So many questions, girl! Was I always—" Rowen stopped, the block hanging in the air between them. "Forgive me, child. You are right to be cautious, but I assure you, you *will* enjoy this."

Rowen took a bite from the corner of the block, snapping a small section with a crack, then chewed. As she uttered a groan of pleasure, she pushed the gift back towards Ella.

Seeing the woman eat, Ella accepted. Following how Rowen had bitten a smaller piece off, she found it solid and cool to the touch. Flavour flooded her mouth, sweet, creamy and amazing. Rowen was right, it possessed a bitter aftertaste, but that just added to the wonder of this food sensation.

"By the light, that's *so* good."

Rowen laughed. "I told you, you'd love it."

"But how did you know?"

Details of the woman's face seemed to form from the darkness of her hood, lips pulled up in a wide grin. "Because I still remember my first time, almost ten years ago."

Ella savoured another bite, chewing slowly. "I've never tasted anything like it."

"It is not of your world, but of mine."

"From the Shade?"

Rowen nodded, her features taking on more definition by the moment, the black skin fading to myriad shades of grey. She squinted at Ella. "What do you see, child?"

"Your face is clearer now. Before it was just darkness."

"Shadowsight is often the first gift to develop. Many more will follow as you become a Shadowmancer, like me."

Ella shook her head. "How is that possible? I have no hue or tone. My sisters all laugh at me, flaunting their subtones. Judath is almost a pure tone, a vibrant red, and she's not afraid to rub my face in it, or anyone else's for that matter. Mother expects her to marry into the nobility."

"That's of no concern anymore, child. Your destiny is for much greater things. It is true you have no talent with the colour, and never will."

Ella's shoulders slumped, her chin falling to rest on her chest.

Rowen reached across, gossamer-thin tendrils of smoke lifting Ella's head until their eyes met. "Do not be ashamed, child. You have something infinitely more powerful. You can weave the shadow, as I do, and that is no minor achievement. Do you realise how many of us become Shadowmancers?"

Ella managed only a slight shake of her head.

"Well, it's less than one in a thousand—fewer than those freaks who *don't* like chocolate!"

Ella chuckled, her cheeks rising. "Thank you for trying to make me feel better."

"This is no attempt to allay your anxiety over worth. You *are* a Shadowmancer, admittedly at the start of your journey, but already on the long path."

"My eyes!"

"Yes, they shall remain dark, as will the rest of your body as you consume the shadow to fuel your craft, but enough talk. We have little time. You must make your choice, and soon."

"What do you mean?"

Rowen lowered her arm for Ella, pulling her up to standing. "You need to take the decisive step. Not slipping and falling into the Gyre, but stepping into it with intention. That will be your true beginning."

Ella frowned. "But you just fished me out of there. I almost drowned."

15

"Yes, but this time you must let it draw you down into the depths and into the Shade willingly. Are you ready?"

Ella's mind flooded with images of what she was about to lose. It took an embarrassingly short time. Her stepmother was too busy matchmaking for her older sisters, especially Judath. All she thought of was how they would become nobility, respectable. She wouldn't have even noticed Ella's absence for the last ten hours. In the two years since her father died, Ella's life had been a nightmare of servitude and beatings. No, she wouldn't miss any of that.

Ella turned, meeting Rowen's eyes. "I'm ready."

Tink clicked his front legs together. "Tink?"

"Oh, what about Tink? I can't leave him."

Rowen laughed again. "Nor would I ask you to. You two seem inseparable."

The woman led Ella to the edge of the silent pool, surface like a black mirror. "Just step forward and open yourself to the Shade. Lock your thoughts into all that is shadow, how I first appeared, the all-encompassing darkness. Focus, child, and we shall meet again on the other side, where your training will begin."

Ella waited, gripping Tink in her quivering hands, filling her mind with all she remembered of the dark. The blackest black, more than just the absence of light, a place which was pure darkness.

With a trembling breath, she forced herself forward, taking the first step into a new destiny.

* * *

The ripples on the pool's surface settled, returning to perfect stillness.

"Tink, tink, tink."

16

Rowen turned, spotting her old construct as he clicked around from his hiding spot, scraping a twisted back leg behind him across the rocky ground.

"Yes," she said, "it does seem just like yesterday."

"Tink?"

"I'm sure she'll be fine." Rowen held a rueful smile for a moment, then it faded into painful memories of her childhood training and loneliness. "She has to be, for all our sakes."

GARETH CLEGG

Gareth lives in make-believe worlds somewhere in the dark spaces between science fiction, horror and fantasy. There he talks with imaginary friends and survives on a diet of tea, scones and the finest curries available to humanity.

His first novel - Fogbound: Empire in Flames - launched on Amazon on 8th Aug 2019 where it rose to become a best seller in the Steampunk Genre. It follows the efforts of a brave group, thrust together to save the British Empire in the wake of the failed Martian invasion of 1895.

Hailing from Huddersfield, in the UK, he enjoys all forms of Speculative fiction. His current project is a series of Weird Western Horror novellas - Chronicles of the Fallen.

To discover more about Gareth and his work, check his Amazon author page **http://Author.to/garethclegg** or his Social Media channels below.

facebook.com/fogbound1899

twitter.com/fogbound1899

instagram.com/fogbound1899

THE CLEEK

"A SCOTTISH BORDER SHERIFF SEEKS TO CAPTURE A MURDEROUS CANNIBAL AND HIS ACCOMPLICES."

IAN F WHITE

Based on a (probably) true story

A devastating plague ravages mainland Europe. Famine follows quickly in its wake.

The British Isles suffers just as badly. At least one third of the population is dead by the middle of the 14th Century, with no end in sight. No family or settlement is spared the misery. Once thriving communities are abandoned as the survivors migrate to what they hope are safer areas.

The Scottish Highlands are thought to be safer than most.

Thought to be...

Lonnie MacKaye sat astride a skinny horse, a mere five feet from the precipice, and looked out over the forested Cairngorm Mountains laid out before him. He scratched at his thick, grey-flecked beard. His tired eyes sensed movement. He smiled and pointed.

"Look, Robbie, over there. Isn't he just the most beautiful thing you've ever seen?"

A young lad of about eight years shifted position on the horse's bare back and stared in the direction his father pointed. His face lit up with excitement when he saw the solitary eagle.

"Aye," Robbie agreed, breathlessly.

A high-pitched scream echoed across the valley, and a second later the bird folded its wings and plummeted out of sight.

"That's the best reason to leave the city; the plague be damned," the man whispered, more to himself than his son.

"Take us back to the wagon, Da, I've got to tell Ma and Aunt Ginny."

The man laughed and nodded. "Right you are, Robbie. Hold on tight now."

As his son gripped him around the waist, the old man clicked his tongue and eased his mount slowly away from the edge and back towards the trail that led to the main path where his young wife and his sister were waiting with the wagon.

The horse moved into the dense woodland at a ponderous, steady walk.

"Da!" Robbie said in exasperation. "Can you no go any faster? We're no pulling the wagon now..."

"Molly's not as young as—" his father began.

Robby slid from the back of the horse, landed squarely on his feet, and was soon sprinting away through the trees.

"... she used to be," the man concluded with a shake of his head. "Watch how you go!" he called out after the lad.

A few minutes later, the horse plodded onto the main path and the rider steered his mount towards the nearby sturdy wagon, piled high with his accrued possessions of forty years as an accomplished furniture maker.

His sister, wife and son were nowhere to be seen. He frowned. With a rough tug on the reins, he brought his horse to a stop. It gave a loud snort of annoyance and shook its matted mane. He lifted his head and took in a deep breath.

The shout that began as his wife's name became a pain-filled scream as an eighteen-inch cast iron hook whistled in over his left shoulder and embedded itself into his ribcage.

Arms flailing wildly, Lonnie's frail form was easily dragged from the horse by the heavily-muscled man who held the pole to which the hook was firmly bound. Another man moved in quickly and drew his bodkin knife across the old man's throat.

As his life gushed away, Lonnie stared into the clear sky above. Something screamed. He hoped it was the eagle's call.

* * *

The Perthshire Reeve, Mathew Russell, looked down at the blood-stained grass and pile of broken furniture lying at the side of the trail. His dark eyes showed no emotion.

"Looks like MacKay's cabinetwork to me," a gruff voice spoke from off to his left.

Russell glanced over at the senior Constable and nodded, "Aye."

His gaze shifted to another man who was crouching at the tree line. The man turned his head, stood and strode over to the Reeve and the Constable.

"They left a trail my Aunt Hetty could follow," the rangy man said.

The Constable grinned, but Russell's expression didn't change.

"How many, Gregor?" Russell asked.

"Two horses, a wagon, and five or six men," the man answered. "We'll have them this time, Matt."

The broad-shouldered Reeve nodded and turned away from the discarded woodwork. He walked towards the seven men – all mounted – who waited on the trail. They weren't soldiers, they were volunteers from Perth, but he had vetted each of them personally. He trusted they would do the job.

One of them held the reins of his own horse. He thanked the man and swung himself into the saddle, adjusting his sword belt to a more comfortable position.

Once the Constable and Gregor had mounted their own steeds, the latter led the way into the trees and the nine men followed on after him in single file.

* * *

The stocky man wore a stiff tan leather apron over his dirty white tunic. It was already spattered with blood yet he still had the old man and the lad to deal with. Fortunately, the women had been a welcome bonus; they were both big 'uns with plenty of meat on their bones.

He grabbed the skinny ankle and lifted the leg almost vertical to the body. Taking his boning knife, he cut away the flesh around the hip and parted sinew and muscle from the joint. He then thrust the point deep between the bones and twisted the leg. There was a sucking noise followed by a crack as Lonnie MacKaye's leg came away from his pelvis. The butcher threw the leg onto a pile of body parts and grabbed a hold of the other leg.

A short man approached the pile, crouched down, and dragged out two arms. He squinted down at the burly butcher. "You had a good haul the other day, Andy."

Andrew Christie looked up. His face and eyes were hard. The hairs on his head and chin were thick and black. He turned his head to one side and blew out his nose before turning back to his gruesome work.

The shorter man stood, shrugged, and walked away – leaving a thin trail of blood as he went – towards the other side of the campsite, where two women were trimming the meat from the bones and rubbing the strips in salt. They looked up briefly, but said nothing.

Everyone's attention was drawn by the arrival of three men who emerged from the trees at the southern edge of the clearing. The new arrivals ignored everyone else and headed straight towards Christie. The women stopped working – the butcher didn't.

The three men halted a few feet from Christie and waited.

Christie finished removing the second leg before he looked up at the men standing before him. They looked back at him nervously. "Peter," he acknowledged the leader of the group.

A bead of sweat ran down Peter's forehead and dripped onto his cheek. He swallowed hard. "Things are getting too dangerous, Andy. The Reeve himself is out looking for us... and Gregor McCauley is with him. We need to move on."

"They'll no find me here," Christie answered calmly. He eyed the other two before looking back at the first. "How much did you make on the horses?"

Peter's hand moved instinctively to the pouch at his waist. "We got a fair price."

"Good."

"We could have used those horses."

"We've discussed that already, Peter." There was menace in Christie's voice, but his manner remained peaceable. "Get back to the watch post."

"But you don't see—"

There was a flash of steel in the morning sunlight. And then all that the onlookers could see of the boning knife was its worn wooden handle – the blade itself buried inside Peter's chest.

Peter took a couple of wobbly steps, his eyes bulging, too shocked to make a sound. He coughed up a mouthful of thick red blood and toppled onto his back. His body spasmed once and then lay still.

The two other men looked from the body lying between them, to each other, and then to Christie's impassive face.

"Are you two of the same mind?" asked the butcher.

"No," they both answered quickly.

"Good. Take the coins to Maggie."

"What about Peter?" one of the men asked, looking down at the body as the other man removed the pouch from Peter's belt.

"Leave him there to drain a while, I'll do him next." Christie reached for another knife.

* * *

Gregor found the old campsite as the sunlight was fading. The hunting party decided to stay there themselves and make a fresh start at dawn.

The mood among the men was still sombre, not helped by the threat of rain from the dark clouds rolling in from the west. And Russell was a hard taskmaster; most of the civilians were having second thoughts about spending any more days away from their families. Fraser, the blacksmith, voiced their concerns to the Constable and he walked over to where Russell and Gregor were discussing the search pattern for tomorrow.

The two men looked at the Constable as he approached.

"What is it, Cal?" asked Russell, seeing the expression on the Constable's face, and the anxious glances of the men seated around the fire a dozen feet away.

Cal blew out his cheeks, "Ach. The men are concerned that we've had nae luck so far. They're wondering how much longer we're likely to be oot here, especially with the weather turning as it is."

Russell nodded. He was surprised they'd lasted so long. "I'll have a word."

The three men walked over to the fire.

Russell glanced at the seated men, one man at a time. Most held his gaze; a couple looked away. His eyes came to rest on the blacksmith.

"The Constable tells me you want to go home," Russell stated.

"Aye," the man replied with a curt nod.

"I'll cut you a deal... One more day, if we don't find them, then we go home. Okay?" He looked over the men again.

One by one, they grudgingly accepted.

"At first light, Gregor and Cal will strike out to the north

28

while the rest of us follow the trail we were following today. It seems to sweep out East, so will actually bring us closer to Perth." A couple of the men made appreciative noises. "Get some sleep."

* * *

Christie was awake – had been for a while – lying on his back, staring up at the dirty cloth of the tent, thinking. He'd followed a strange path the last six months, but didn't regret any of it; leaving his shop in Perth, getting lost in the hills, joining this group of misfits, and taking over after he'd killed their previous leader in a fair fight. Well, it hadn't exactly been fair. He'd used the hook on the man, the tool that had given rise to the nickname the others used behind his back; *The Cleek*.

But he finally had to admit it to himself; he'd grown tired of it all, the killing and cannibalism. Maybe it was time for a change after all. There was only one thing about this part of his life he hadn't tired of.

To his left, Maggie lay beside him under the sheets. She was warm. He shuffled over onto one elbow and watched her for a while. Still in her prime; beautiful; long brown hair, perfect breasts, and wide hips.

"Maggie?" he whispered, reaching over and gently stroking her hair.

She stirred and opened her eyes a crack. "What?" she replied, sleepily.

"Ever been to Dumfries?"

"Eh?" she blinked a couple of times. "No... Why?" She was wide awake now. "What plan are you scheming now?"

"I've had enough. It's time we moved on. I'll send the others out to the watch posts and then we'll leave."

"After what you said to Peter?" she sat up and looked at him,

29

a frown creasing her forehead. Her hair fell down over her shoulders and the front of her pale nightshirt.

Christie looked away for a second. "Aye, well, I changed my mind." He turned back. "Is that all right with you, your ladyship?"

She smiled mischievously at him. "You know I'll go anywhere with you, and your meat, my big butcher." She pulled at the bottom of her shirt and climbed astride him, but he held her back. Her brow furrowed again.

"I need to pee," he grinned.

* * *

Glenn and Mary walked the two miles to their watch post on the Perth road in silence, each lost in their own thoughts.

Glenn considered himself one of the original group that had decided to supplement their diets with human flesh, waylaying and killing unwary travellers. He had initially welcomed Christie and the skills he brought to the group, but just lately, he'd felt the big butcher was taking over, and if anyone was to take over, it should be he, not Christie. He'd kill Christie tonight and take Maggie for a ride over his dead body, and then kill her too. He smiled at the thought.

Mary saw the smile and correctly interpreted the gist of her companion's thoughts. She was content with things as they were; she trusted Christie and was happy for him to lead. She might tell him of her suspicions of Glenn. Maybe she could even persuade him to tarry a while with her in his bed – when that bitch Maggie wasn't around.

They had just reached the road when they heard the horses and saw the group of men in the woods. The lead rider saw them at the same moment, and raised a hand.

Glenn replied in kind and angled his head towards Mary.

"Keep your head, Mary. They don't know who we are, no need to give them cause to—"

Mary turned and ran.

"Stupid bitch!" Glenn cursed, and ran after her.

The horsemen yelled and urged their mounts forward, grateful for the change in pace, their earlier misgivings forgotten. Their horse's hooves drummed loud and wet on the sodden earth of the road.

Mary glanced back in time to see Glenn close behind, reaching out a hand for her. There was murder in his eyes. She yelped in alarm and ducked, changing direction, his hand swiping the air above her head.

Glenn was not near as nimble as she was, managing to entangle his own feet in the undergrowth beside the trail, and fell sprawling on his face in the mud.

Mary took a second to spit on her would-be assailant, before turning again and pushing her way into the relative safety of the trees. Those men would not be able to follow on horseback, and she was confident she could outrun them; all four of them were large and cumbersome-looking.

Glenn rolled aside and got to his feet as he heard the approaching riders. In a flash, he had his bodkin in hand and a snarl on his lips. He dodged around the first horse, drawing his knife down the thigh of its rider. The man yelled in pain. Glenn let out a triumphant shout, but a second later the blacksmith's iron-shod stave cracked his skull open with one stroke. Glenn fell dead, his blood and brains mixing with the watery mud.

"Tom, get after her!" Fraser shouted. "And someone bind my leg."

Tom sprang from his horse and gave chase.

Mary was correct; knowing the woods well, she easily outpaced the man pursuing her. Within minutes, she could no longer hear him crashing through the undergrowth. She slowed her pace and altered her direction, aiming back towards the camp. Christie needed to know about Glenn and the horsemen.

She had gone no more than a hundred and fifty yards when a man suddenly stepped out from behind a tree. His back was to her, but she flinched and let out an involuntary squeal.

He turned to look at her, one hand still straightening his codpiece, the other already resting on the hilt of his broadsword. Mary stared at him. He was broad-shouldered, tall, and looked as mean as a bastard.

"Shit!" she hissed.

"Hello, miss," he spoke in a low tone. "Who—"

Mary panicked again and backed away, ready to run. She backed into a tree. No, not a tree... another man! She turned to stare into the clean-shaven face of a youth. He had beautiful blue eyes and a mop of shoulder-length blonde hair. He looked like an angel.

"Hold her," the first man ordered.

"Aye, Mister Russell," the lad said, grabbing Mary by the upper arms.

She sagged in his grasp – her spirit broken – and began to sob uncontrollably. "Please don't kill me. I know where he is. I'll take you there. Don't kill me."

The two men shared a look. Russel allowed himself a grim smile.

Gregor and Cal rode closer to the copse of trees and bushes.

They slowed and then halted about twenty feet away.

"It was aboot here," the Constable said to the tracker in a harsh whisper. He turned back to look at the trees and raised his voice. "I know you're in there – I saw you from the other side of the clearing. Come on oot now."

There was no response.

Gregor raised an eyebrow. "Doesn't sound like there's anyone here, Cal."

"I saw a woman; she wore a light blue dress," Cal replied. "Hold my horse."

Cal handed his reins to Gregor and dismounted. With one hand resting on the hilt of his sword, he approached the trees. "I know you're in there. Come on oot now; I'm a Constable from Perth."

He'd taken no more than a half dozen steps when there was a noise from ahead and a woman parted the foliage and stepped out. She held a bundle of clothes in front of her and her head was lowered, eyes firmly on the ground.

Cal looked over his shoulder and grinned up at Gregor. "Told ye."

Gregor grinned back and shook his head. A noise in the grass behind him made him turn around. Cal heard it too. There was no-one there, just a stone rolling to a stop in the grass.

The woman quickly closed the distance to the Constable, drawing out a meat cleaver as she did so. Cal turned in time to see the blade and threw up an arm to protect his head as she struck. He shrieked as the heavy blade sheared through the cloth of his tunic sleeve and cut deep into the bones of his forearm. The force was enough to crack them both. He staggered backwards, reaching for his own weapon.

Gregor's head whipped around at the cry and he saw a man lurching out of the trees, a wicked-looking hook on the end of a pole held in his hands. The man was fast, but Gregor was quicker – he rolled from his saddle and managed to draw his sword before the other reached him.

Maggie stepped in closer to the Constable, pinning his sword arm against his body. She was stronger than he'd anticipated. The second blow came down in the crook of his

33

neck. Blood sprayed, soaking them both in hot, sticky fluid. She let go of him and he sank to his knees. Kicking him over, she looked to see how Christie was faring with the other one.

Gregor leaped back to avoid the sweep of the cleek and darted in to catch Christie in the throat with the point of his blade. The big butcher parried the blade with his wooden pole and swung his weapon at the tracker's legs.

Gregor quickly jumped up to avoid the polearm and came down with one foot on the curve of the hook. Christie twisted the pole and the point of the hook ripped through the tracker's thick leggings, gouging a deep scratch in his calf. But for a second, Gregor had control. Setting his jaw against the searing pain in his leg, he lifted his weapon ready to strike.

Maggie brought the cleaver down on Gregor's head. There was a loud crack and her victim fell dead at her feet. She smiled at Christie and then followed his gaze to the front of her dress. "Ah, yes, I need to change."

While Maggie changed and then stripped the two bodies of useful items, Christie rounded up the horses. And then they resumed their journey towards Dumfries.

* * *

It was a late autumn market day in Dumfries. The night's frost was still glistening on cobbles and rooftops around the town. Even at this early hour there were many stallholders and customers about.

Russell stood in an alleyway off the main square. Four guardsmen lurked in the shadows behind him. He had a dozen more concealed in other locations. They all wore steel helms and mail shirts under their tunics, a precaution he hoped would save their lives. His mood darkened even more as he recalled the sight of Gregory and the Constable. That bastard, Andrew Christie, wouldn't get away this time.

On the other side of the marketplace, he could see Maggie Murray tending the butcher's stall. She conversed easily with her customers. If only they knew of her past deeds. He guessed they'd all come to her hanging.

He could also see the infamous cleek itself hanging from iron brackets fixed to the stall behind her. That was a bold and foolhardy move, and one that had confirmed their identity.

In the two years since the execution of the cannibals he'd captured, their leader had escaped the Reeve's every attempt to locate him, and his murderous mistress bitch. The breakthrough had come a week earlier, with reports of a sighting of the pair in Dumfries. Now that the worst of the plague was over, and people were returning to the towns again, he had more eyes and ears to rely upon.

And now here he was, waiting for Christie to make his appearance. Then he would spring his trap. He wanted to take the butcher alive, so he could suffer before he was hung, drawn and quartered in Perth.

A tall, thick-set man walked into the square, sweat glistening on his bald head. He pushed a small two-wheeled cart, upon which were piled the recently slaughtered carcasses of a pig and two sheep. He had a couple of days' worth of stubble, but no beard.

"That's him," Russell growled. "Come on."

Without waiting for an answer, the Reeve strode out into the square. The four men hurried to keep pace. Around the marketplace, similarly clad guardsmen saw Russell and his companions move out. They began to close the net.

Christie saw Maggie had already opened up the stall and was selling off yesterday's leftovers. He grinned. This year, they'd produce a bairn or two. His smile slipped when he saw the guardsmen moving towards the stall.

"Maggie!" he called out.

She saw him and waved. Then she saw the guardsmen and reached for her cleaver.

"Andrew Christie?" someone said from close by.

Christie turned his head slowly, as if in a daze. He saw Russell and his men. He frowned.

"Take him," said Russell, stepping aside for the guardsmen. They moved forward, cudgels in hand.

Christie burst into action. He grabbed a hold of the hind legs of a sheep and swung it around in a wide arc with as much power as he was able. He took down three of the men with his first swing and then threw the carcass at the fourth soldier.

Russell was knocked off-balance by the last man as he staggered under the blow from the sheep carcass. Both men maintained their feet, but were unable to instantly pursue Christie as he turned and ran into the crowd of onlookers.

Christie heard Maggie scream his name a couple of times in between curses and the yells of the guardsmen. And then she fell silent. Out of the corner of his eye, he saw her on the ground, curled up into a ball as clubs and kicks rained down on her. That was a shame, but he had to take care of himself now.

He barged a couple of people aside and sprinted towards a nearby street. Two guards barred his way so he changed direction, skidding a little on the slick cobbles, and ran for another alley. He saw more guards. There were too many. He had to find another way out.

"Stop him!" yelled Russell as he righted himself and gave chase. The market was only two streets away from the river. If Christie made it there, he'd doubtless escape again. Russell redoubled his efforts to catch up with his prey.

Christie weighed up his options as he ran. He had no

transport; they'd sold the horses upon arrival in the town in order to finance the market stall. Maybe he could steal a horse, but that would take time. His best option would be to reach the river, but he was penned in the square. A quick glance up at the roofs, and a new plan was formed.

A nearby clothier's stall was backed against the wall of a sturdy stone building, the roof of which could easily be reached from the stall's awning. Decision made, Christie leaped onto the stall, scattering bundles of cloth onto the ground as he climbed.

"Stop him!" Russell shouted again, adding "Idiots," under his breath as he saw three guardsmen halt at the base of the wall and just stand and watch as Christie clambered onto the steep tiled roof.

"Get out of the way," he ordered as he skidded to a halt. The men parted and he leaped onto the stall and gave chase.

The footing on the roof was treacherous; Christie's feet slipped, and he almost fell twice as he hurried up the slope to the ridge and down the other side. He could hear someone panting hard as they followed after him. Guessing it was the commander of the guardsmen, he risked a look. Sure enough, seconds later the man's head rose above the ridgeline.

Russell took a moment to look down at the guardsmen standing at the base of the wall. "Are you men witless?" he called back at them, "Go around, you fools. Go around." He gesticulated with one arm, the other clinging tightly to the decorated ridge tiles.

Christie stood on the eaves and crouched low, and then he sprang, reaching for the roof of a lower neighbouring house. Landing awkwardly, he soon gained a secure grasp in the thatch and began to pull himself up. Again, his slick-soled boots skidded on the damp reeds as he hurried to gain purchase. Arriving at the ridge, he looked out over the broad river Nith a mere two yards away, and grinned.

Russell followed after his quarry, landing in roughly the same place, and managed to grab a hold of the other man's ankle. Christie yelped, more in surprise than pain, and kicked out with his other leg. The Reeve gritted his teeth, hanging on tightly and reaching for his dagger.

Christie stared down at his pursuer dangling from his leg. He was a tenacious bastard this one. Drawing his other foot up, he readied his blow for when the man's head came closer. He saw the flash of steel and felt the awful pain before he could do anything about it.

Russell pinned the butcher's leg to the roof with his dagger and used it to pull himself forward. With a cry of absolute rage, Christie swung his free foot out and upwards. The point of his boot connected with Russell's chin, slid into his throat and dislocated his jaw.

Russell's eyes rolled up in their sockets and his body went limp. His grip loosened and he slid down the roof, and seconds later, fell off the edge.

With a strength and resolve borne of desperation, Christie grasped the hilt of the dagger and dragged it out of his leg. Blood soaked into his boot. Using the dagger to aid his own climb, he soon made it to the ridge, rolled over, and slid down the other side. He too fell off the roof, but he landed in the river with a loud splash, and was carried away on the strong current.

Russell lay on his back in the cobbled alley, staring up at the cloud laden sky. He could not move, presuming his spine was broken. He also felt an increasing pain at the back of his head. The faces of the guardsmen crowded around him. A strange feeling of peace washed over him, though his task remained incomplete. He was going to be with his Rosie. His blood pooled on the cobbles around his head, his eyes glazed and his life ebbed away.

Christie crawled out of the river, dragged himself onto the

bank and rolled over onto his back. As he stared up at the cloud laden sky, a beautiful face moved into view.

"Are you all right, mister?" the young woman asked, crouching down beside him and placing a hand gently on his arm.

"Aye, I think so. I fell into the river." He rolled onto one elbow and looked down at his leg. "I... hurt my leg." He stared at the tight bodice and then up into the girl's large round eyes and he smiled. "Can you help me to my feet, miss? Do you live nearby? My name's Andrew..."

IAN F WHITE

Ian F White has been sharing his story-telling creations since the mid-1980s, initially in the form of roleplaying and wargaming scenarios, but more recently as regular literary work. He currently has more than ten titles available, mostly concerning the Action & Adventure genre with occasional  jaunts into Horror, Fantasy, Science-Fiction, and Comedy.

He lives in Huddersfield, West Yorkshire, with his mutually devoted wife, and cats.

You can find out more at his
    Amazon Author's Page: **author.to/Ian-F-White**
    or on his Website **https://wyvernebg.webs.com/**

THE CHEAT CODE

"A SCI-FI STORY THAT FOLLOWS A MAN WHO SEES A VISION DURING EARTH'S LAST HOURS."

CM ANGUS

"And there it is."

Adam glanced across at his wife, her words still in the air, still distracting him. He looked out from his porch to the rest of his neighbourhood in complete darkness and eerie silence.

It was the same on every street. It was the same in every town and city. It was the same all over the planet.

Had it really only been yesterday that the news channels had run the story? Fox, CNN, RT, BBC: all of them alerting the world of an imminent solar storm; the biggest since the Carrington event in 1859.

Back then, there hadn't been the grid; there hadn't been the internet; there hadn't been anything really, but there had still been problems.

Back then, electrons from that solar flare had found telegraph wires and caused huge surges – in some cases electrocuting operators and setting fire to paper in their telegraph offices.

This time it wouldn't only be telegraph lines that would burn.

This time it would be different.

This time it would be worse.

If any satellites survived, it would be a miracle. Only God knew what lay in store.

As far as possible, all infrastructure on the ground had been segmented or disconnected to try to offer some level of protection. For the first time in over a hundred years, the world was to be powered down.

Adam watched as street lamps were extinguished like dominoes toppling, and, save for the few nominated medical centres around the world, everything was still.

He gently squeezed his wife with the arm that was already over her shoulder and felt the soft touch of Tasmin's own arm around his waist squeezing back.

And there it was.

Adam took a sip of the coffee he'd made earlier and breathed in the stillness.

It wasn't that they were in total darkness – many of his neighbours had flashlights or candles – it was more a sense of total peacefulness that not only washed over him, but over everyone and everything.

Toby, their ever-frantic German shepherd, lay silent and still, out of character for him, and though it was a warm night, not even a single chirp of a cricket could be heard.

But the most wondrous part was not the silence. It was the sky.

For the first time ever, Adam looked to the night sky and saw the whole universe stretch out beyond the horizon, saw the sides of the valley strike silhouettes against the canvas of the stars.

The strangest thing, however, was that it wasn't dark, it was perfectly clear and the Milky Way's blanket of colours shone out purples, blues and hues of gold.

It was not just beautiful – the scale was immense.

Adam looked up and he looked out. He gazed into the expanse and suddenly felt insignificantly tiny. He saw the Earth against the infinite scale of creation, and in that transparent instant, he saw it all.

Jobbing supply teacher, Adam Mynott, suddenly felt a mix of euphoria, disconnection and calm. Looking down, he saw himself in his front yard arm in arm with his wife. He saw his neighbourhood and community far below him. He saw his country and he saw his world.

In his mind's eye he saw the Earth, the galaxy and in an instant, he understood everything.

Everything...

He could not put it into words, but it was as if a secret had been revealed, as if he'd been given the key.

"Can you see it?" he asked his wife.

"See what?"

"The message," he replied. "The message to the world."

Tasmin furrowed her brow and looked sideways at her husband.

"There you go with your hippy bullshit again," she muttered under her breath.

If Adam was aware of her disapproval, he did not show it. Instead he continued to stare out into the night and to withdraw further into himself.

Tasmin's thoughts might be true, but he was elsewhere. He suddenly knew how it all worked.

All of it.

He saw the universe like he'd never seen it before. He saw the levers, the triggers and he saw the back doors. He saw the secrets of existence and all the inner workings of life itself.

He saw the cheat-code needed to manipulate reality – and saw everything, all at once.

He knew real magic.

Adam stretched out and flexed his mind. He felt an ancient power resonate deep within him. It was like the Earth's electrical backbone and its harsh artificial light had deadened the subtlety required to support magic.

It was as if, with all that the world had gained from its technological advances, it had lost its way. The spectacular had become humdrum and humanity had become adrift from its true place in the universe.

It was only now that the deafening silence and calm allowed the old ways to resurface. Humanity, once again, contemplated its place amongst the stars, and billions of eyes turned to the sky to wonder at the face of God.

A collective wonder that could be harnessed.

Adam reached deep within himself and stretched his mind

towards the stars. He saw the solar storm growing in intensity, bearing down upon the Earth.

I can protect it.

Turning toward Tasmin, he looked straight through her. "There's something I've got to do."

As his wife looked on, he *manifested an intention* like never before. His fingers traced strange shapes, and under his breath he heard his voice whisper incantations in a hoarse unworldly-tongue.

The layer of protection that he cast infused and enveloped the world. It didn't so much shield the Earth from the incoming storm as make it immune to its effects.

The invisible wave front of solar flares washed in, but rather than causing the destruction that had been predicted, it came and it went without event. It passed through the Earth, the satellites, and everything else without effect.

Exhausted but finally satisfied, Adam leant back on the rail of his porch and drew deeply on the now cold coffee.

It was done.

Now that he knew the secret, nothing would ever be the same.

But for now, he needed rest.

Tomorrow...

Adam awoke the next day to the sound of his radio alarm clock. He reached over to swipe it to snooze, but paused as he began to pick up parts of the conversation on the talk-radio station.

"...complete waste of time..."

"...how did the scientists get it so wrong?"

"...I'm not complaining, but they said this was going to be a global disaster."

"...yet more scaremongering."

Adam Mynott came round and, recalling the events of the night before, reached out with his mind.

Nothing.

Where there had been magic and understanding, there was now the mundane reality that had always been there.

Had it all just been a dream?

He would have asked Tasmin, but she'd already left for work. All was as normal as it had ever been and at the bottom of his bed Toby still slept.

The radio in the background suddenly attracted his attention.

"...Yes it was very strange," a NASA spokesman was heard to say. "The intensity of the flares should have been catastrophic, but as far as we can tell, they had no effect. At the minute we're still analysing what this means, but this could change our whole understanding of science."

"And the reason that you're on the show today," the presenter interjected, "is that you're asking listeners to get in touch if they experienced anything during the storm. Is that right?"

"That's right, Fred. As you say, we want people to share with us their experiences of the storm so we can build up a picture of what happened..."

* * *

"Thanks for coming at such short notice, Adam. Please sit down."

Since calling them an hour earlier, Adam had been surprised at just how rapidly they'd sent a car to fetch him. He hadn't even finished talking on the phone when the car pulled up.

Not even enough time to call Tasmin.

He'd arrived at an unassuming office block with no signage

and was shown into a windowless room where an engineer already sat.

Glasses, short-sleeved patterned shirt and a poorly chosen tie. Apart from the absence of a pocket protector, what else could he be?

The room was bare, save for strip lights, table and spartan metal chairs.

The engineer spoke but did not get up.

"Thanks for coming at such short notice, Adam. Please sit down."

Feeling uncomfortable, Adam nervously took the free seat.

"You said you stopped the storm?"

Adam was stunned by the directness of the question.

What had he even said earlier?

Much of last night now felt like a dream.

"To tell you the truth, I don't know what I believe any more," he said. "Last night when the power went off was like nothing I've ever felt before... The stars... It was like we'd all seen the face of God. And all I did was channel that feeling of wonder."

Adam tried to explain that he'd been able to see everything in infinite clarity, that he'd been able to perform what he could only call magic, that he'd caused the storm to pass unhindered.

But that was last night.

Today it had gone.

Today, he was just an average Joe.

To what extent they took him seriously he didn't know. They wrote it all down, thanked him for his time and then ushered him back to the car.

And just like that it was over.

In the nights that followed he'd sit on his porch and look at the stars, but instead of a blanket of wonder there were simply the constellations that everyone with a passing familiarity with the zodiac knew.

Life went on, of course, but it was never the same. He

struggled to ride the subway or even venture out. The sight of thousands of humans glued to their smartphones depressed him too much.

If only they could, once again, collectively look to the stars.

Had it really happened? Did magic really exist? Had the rise of technology and an inability to gaze out into their universe replaced the magical with the mundane?

The world was full of spiritual beings but none of them knew it.

They could be so much more...

CM ANGUS

Born and raised in a steel-town in the Northeast of England, CM Angus now lives in Yorkshire with his better half, his children and an awesome dog.

With a background in e-Commerce and technology, his work is inquisitive and blends a passion for story telling with a strong scientific grounding. He is currently working on Fixpoint, a series of books with each piece tackling different aspects of discontinuities in time and is a Speculative Fiction spanning 4 generations of a family haunted by the prospect of an approaching alternate reality where their child has been erased from history.

Overstrike, Volume 1 of Fixpoint, was published by Elsewhen Press in 2020.

Follow CM Angus at https://cmangus.blogspot.com or via his Social Media Channels.

amazon.com/author/cmangus

facebook.com/author.cm.angus

twitter.com/c_m_angus

instagram.com/author.cm.angus

goodreads.com/cm_angus

RAVENING DARKNESS

"AN ANGRY STUDENT SUMMONS A HELLISH
BEAST, UNLEASHING DEATH AND
DESTRUCTION ON THE EARTH."

NICK STEAD

Flashes of gunfire tore holes in the darkness just as bullets tore through flesh. Then the shadows came rushing back in, like a weight pressing against the eyes. Screams of the fallen rang through the night; cries not just of pain but also of terror and pleas for help. And still men continued to fire blindly, killing friend and foe alike in the endless spray, but always missing the true enemy, the cause of this bloody massacre.

Those screams began to die and guns quietened, the deadly hail of bullets coming to a halt at last. Somewhere nearby a solitary voice called for his mother. Like countless others before him, the man begged for help that would not come, until he was cut off with an awful finality. Silence descended, and the land was still.

Yet even in this place of death and destruction there was still life, if not hope. Shell-shocked and dazed, Johnny got to his feet, too stunned to feel the shame of his cowardice – that would come much later. And if the others had seen what he'd seen, would they have acted any differently? Or would their courage have failed them, as his had? But they hadn't seen, and by the time they'd realised they faced more than just enemy soldiers, it had already been too late. Now they lay dead, their courage buying nothing but a painful end. And he lived on.

Some part of him was aware he couldn't stay there, cowering in the dirt and shivering with more than just twilight's chill, so he took his first shaky step, and then another and another, arms outstretched like a blind man. It was slow going. The woods had seemed like the perfect place to seek shelter, but navigating through the trees was proving a challenge – one which could very well be his undoing.

The sound of his own rapid heartbeat filled the silence as he walked, nerves taut and belly sick with fear. Death's foul perfume was heavy on the air, the stench of blood and worse thick in his nostrils, and soon his boots began to squelch through pools of what he knew to be that same crimson fluid. It seemed he had not been the only one to desert his post after all, though the others had apparently not fared so well. He was going to have to reach civilisation before the thing found him if he didn't want to meet the same fate, and so he staggered on, stumbling across the uneven ground.

A loop of something caught in a tree branch brushed his face, like a vine hanging down except this was no jungle, and he'd never touched any kind of plant life that warm and slimy. An involuntary whimper escaped his throat with the realisation of what it must be. Already nauseous, he couldn't fight the foul stream of bile which rose up in response, and he fell to his knees.

Johnny retched until his stomach was empty. Fresh fear rolled over him at the thought that the noise of it might attract the living nightmare stalking the shadows, but he could hear no hint of that dread presence approaching. No attack came as he got back to his feet, body trembling more violently with each reluctant step. Part of him just wanted to curl up amongst the tree roots again and pray the creature didn't find him, rather than continue along this path which had surely descended into Hell. His progress grew even slower, and several times he almost tripped over what he tried to imagine were fallen logs, not the grisly remains of once brave men left to rot in the dirt.

A hand grabbed his ankle. He screamed in response, while a voice high with pain and terror garbled something at him in a foreign language. Johnny fought to break free of the German soldier's grip, succeeding as the last reserves of the other man's strength died away.

His thoughts turned to the girl waiting for him back home. Oh how they'd dreamed the dreams of youth, intending to marry and start a family someday, when the war was over. Had he thrown it all away in this dumb quest to seek honour and glory? It seemed so meaningless now. If only someone had told him the truth of the life he'd chosen, perhaps he might not have been so quick to run off to battle, head filled with foolish thoughts of medals awarded for brave deeds and being hailed a hero of his country. But there was no glory on the battlefield, only death and pain, even without the unnatural horror coming for him.

With a whimper, he realised that horror was already closing in. Two pinpricks of red glowed in the darkness, blazing with an otherworldly malice greater even than the cruelty of men. Johnny thought of his comrades, and for one crazy moment he fancied their spirits might return to save him and avenge themselves. But no one was coming to rescue him. No one was coming to see to it that he would escape with his life, back home to his sweet Mary who he was never going to see again. All alone, he clutched his gun.

Strobe lighting split the gloom in psychedelic flashes, decades later. A mass of bodies danced and swayed in the dimly lit confines of the club, packed in so tightly it was impossible to move through the crowd without spilling a few drinks here and there. Connor watched the scene unfold as another girl reached for the outstretched hand of what could only be described as a god. He pulled her up onto one of four raised platforms to join the other women dancing there, all vying for his attention.

Connor didn't know who the guy was but he wished he possessed whatever power the dude had over the girls in this place. What he wouldn't give to be surrounded by a throng of female bodies swaying suggestively around him in a kind of worship. That's exactly what they were doing for the stranger; as if he were part of the band they were dancing to, and the platform his stage.

Attempting to follow suit, Connor climbed onto a different 'stage' and played some air guitar in an attempt to look cool. A dark-haired beauty dancing nearby caught his eye and he held out his hand to her in invitation, just as he'd seen the other man do time and again that night. The girl shook her head and manoeuvred herself back into the tightly knit throng, leaving him wondering what the hell he was doing wrong. He might not have as muscular a body as the 'god' with his harem of chicks, but he wasn't unattractive or awkward either. So why was it they only had eyes for the new guy?

He danced till the end of the song, when he was forced to admit it looked like this was another lost cause. The beer wasn't even giving him that nice pleasant buzz he would usually be enjoying on a Saturday night, and the music was only okay at best. It was the right genre but none of his favourite bands. So Connor jumped back down and headed to the bar for a last drink. Unless he suddenly got lucky there was nothing more for him here, but perhaps just one more pint would give him the buzz he craved. Then he would call it a night.

* * *

On the street outside the rock club, Shane was losing his temper with his current girlfriend, Chantelle, and Josh wasn't helping matters.

"Bitch, we're not going back yet so shut yer gob," he said.

"OMG you did not just call me bitch and if we can't go back yet can we at least go somewhere else; fucking freezing out here," she replied, barely pausing for breath.

He was about to reply when he noticed some random guy on the other side of the road staring at them.

"What the fuck are you looking at? You starting on me, mate? Are yer fucking starting on me? No? Didn't think so, yer twat," he shouted. To Chantelle, with little sincerity, he said "Sorry, babe, I didn't mean it. We'll go find somewhere playing some real tunes, not this mosher shit they're playing in there. And look, I got you this."

He reached into his pocket as Josh mumbled "I still think this is a bad idea, mate."

"You wanna shut yer gob an' all. What's wrong with you tonight? Stop being such a pussy," he said, pulling out the smartphone he'd swiped from some idiot stupid enough to leave it poking out of a jacket pocket. "Here yer go, babe, got this for yer."

"OMG is that a Sony Xperia? Oh, Shane!" she cried, throwing her arms around him and giving him a kiss.

Her whining temporarily averted, they moved on to find somewhere with more mainstream club music. Josh still felt uneasy about the stolen phone, though he couldn't explain why. It wasn't like it was the first thing he and Shane had nicked, but for some reason his gut was telling him this phone was trouble. And a rough childhood had taught him to listen to his gut.

* * *

They were just about to serve him at the bar when Connor had the sudden panicked realisation that the weight of his phone was gone from his jacket. He willed it to be his imagination as he felt frantically in each of his pockets, but no, it had indeed gone.

Connor swore and fought his way through the crowd of club goers all waiting to be served, scanning the floor in the hopes it had simply dropped out and would be lying there, waiting for him to pick it up. But there was no sign of it round the bar area. He thought perhaps he could have lost it while he'd been playing air guitar and waded his way back through the sea of drunks, his progress hampered by the press of bodies bumping into him with every step. It didn't matter which way he moved, the current always seemed to be against him in the alcoholic tide of happy thoughtlessness, people dancing across his path without a care in the world.

"Hey, watch it," a guy said with beer-fuelled aggression, proving the tide could turn at any moment. Connor mumbled an apology and continued his search, hampered even further by the unnatural light of the dance floor. He'd been round the club three times before he accepted he was not going to find his beloved phone among the ever shifting forest of unsteady feet. If it was still in the building it had either been picked up already or kicked out of sight. And either way, he was not going to find it in there that night.

Defeated and upset, he stepped out of the club just as it started to rain. Connor could not help but feel lost without that expensive device the modern world relied so heavily on, and for a brief moment he had the strange, sorrowful sensation of having lost a close friend. After all, a phone was no longer just a phone. There were all those memories stored on there in the form of pictures and video files, and contacts he would have a hard time getting hold of again, which he'd foolishly never bothered to back up. It had held a part of his life, and now it was gone.

Connor raised his face towards the sky, as if beseeching help from the heavens. The rain was cold on his bare skin, but he just stood there for several minutes, thinking back over the night's events and replaying his memories. A glimmer of hope rekindled when he realised he'd not actually had his phone out in that place. Could it have fallen from his pocket before he'd even got there? He'd definitely had it in the bar prior to that because he'd been texting one of his mates, but that was the last time he remembered having it. So he retraced his steps, searching the street as he went. But again his search was in vain, and the bar itself was now closed. There was every chance some bastard had picked it up and pocketed it already, and his hope withered into despair again. It really was gone, probably for good.

Sadness turned to anger as he walked back to his student flat. How could he have been so careless? He'd carried his old brick around for five long years without ever once misplacing it, and then the moment he'd decided to shell out for a smartphone and treat himself to the latest technology, he'd managed to lose it within two months. It wasn't even like he could blame the alcohol, still feeling far too clear headed. He should have zipped his pocket to keep it secure instead of risking walking around with it open out of sheer laziness, and now he was paying the price for his poor judgement.

He was too busy beating himself up to notice he was being followed. The 'god' had watched as Connor searched the club, before rushing off to look outside. He'd disentangled himself from the net of dancing female bodies he'd surrounded himself with, their disappointment plain to see. In truth they were no more than a cover to help him blend in, his heart already claimed by another, and besides, it was duty that had called him here, and he took his duty seriously.

He knew exactly what lurked on the fringes of this reality, never content in its own domain, always watching from the shadows and searching for a way back in. It was getting closer to crossing back into the mortal plane for the first time in decades, he could feel it, and somehow Connor was central to its return, though whether the boy's role was sacrificial or as a summoner the 'god' wasn't yet sure. All he could do was shadow the student's movements and wait for the time to intervene. Then he would do whatever it took to prevent anything that could possibly summon the thing stalking the darkness, even if that meant taking a life to save millions. So he followed Connor back to his flat and took cover in a nearby hedgerow, knowing that at least when it did happen it could only be during the night, so that gave him the daylight hours to rest. But while the sun was down he would watch and he would wait, and he would be ready.

* * *

Sunlight streamed through the thin fabric of his curtains, calling Connor back to the land of the living. Groaning with tiredness, he groped for his phone, confused when his questing fingers felt only the wood of the bedside table and scraps of paper which he would get round to sorting through and binning, one of these days. The events of the previous night crashed back into place and he threw back the covers, jumping up and running straight for the landline.

First he tried the rock club to see if his phone had been handed in, but the staff member told him the only lost property this weekend was a woman's coat and a set of keys. Next he tried the bar where he'd definitely last had it, but they'd found nothing at all. Finally he tried the police and reported it stolen, though he held little hope that they would find the thief and recover it for him. They were already overworked and understaffed, and a stolen phone would be among the lowest of their priorities.

After the police he rang his network provider to block the phone so at least its new owner couldn't get the full use out of it. If only he'd bothered with PIN protection, maybe the thief would have handed it in when they'd found it was going to be little more than an expensive paperweight to them. But his model hadn't come with that feature automatically turned on and he'd never taken the time to turn it on himself. Nor had he bothered with its GPS security features. When he was finished on the landline he booted up his laptop and trawled the net for information about tracking stolen mobiles, but with the GPS off it proved just as fruitless as his other efforts.

Having done all he could, Connor supposed he should make a start on some of the coursework he'd allowed to pile up. He typed in the URL for one of the recommended reading sites they'd been given and started his research into land use and regulation. It was a dull subject at the best of times and his least favourite module in Law so far, but that day he was having an even harder time concentrating than usual. His thoughts kept straying to the twat who'd nabbed his phone, oddly faceless in his imagination like the blurring on TV used to protect people's identity. No doubt they were enjoying all its apps, slowly erasing the pieces of his life in favour of their own. The horrible thought that his music library was probably being replaced even as he sat there trying to work rooted itself in his brain, growing stronger with every passing moment until it seemed to fill his skull so that he could think of little else. Was all his precious rock and metal being erased to make room for dance and hip-hop?

Anger took hold once more, killing the last of his concentration. Connor found himself wanting to take justice into his own hands, but what more could he do without knowing who had taken possession of the phone and where they lived? The town he now called home was large enough that it could have been anyone – a needle in a haystack as the old saying went. Without some kind of starting point, some clue as to where to look, he was powerless to act and he knew it. Unless...

What was that site he'd come across when he'd been researching the 'Evil' module last term? It had been some kind of occult thing dedicated to the dark arts. And much as he wanted to believe in the paranormal, he'd been sceptical when he'd first visited it, dismissing the spells as no more than fanciful verses written by a satanic wannabe. Yet there'd been something about the webpages that had made him uneasy. Something that had made his hairs stand on end, though he'd not wanted to admit it to himself at the time.

Now he found himself accepting that there might be something more to it than that after all. And if there was even the slightest chance one of those spells could work, was it not worth a try? Black magic might not be able to bring him his phone back, but maybe it could give him some satisfaction in the belief that whoever had taken it was suffering for their crime.

"Come on, it has to be in my browsing history somewhere," he muttered to himself, tapping away at his keyboard as he tried various different words and phrases in the 'search history' box. After scrolling through countless URLs, finally he found the one he wanted and clicked to open the site.

From the moment it loaded, an unseen force seemed to brush across his skin, raising the hairs once again. His heart quickened as his mouse hovered over 'Curses' in the navigation bar, thinking that was probably what he wanted for revenge on someone. But there was another link for 'Demons, Devils and Other Dark Entities' which he felt himself drawn to, for reasons he could not quite put into words.

Clicking the link brought up a page with a list of what appeared to be names, and one in particular caught his eye, though again he could not say why. Connor clicked that link and found himself looking at a summoning ritual resonating with power, as if the very words on the screen had an energy to them, even before they were spoken aloud. The tingling on his skin grew more intense and his heart began to beat faster still, his nerve almost failing him then. But the thought of some bastard walking round with what was rightfully his was all it took to keep him reading the instructions and the incantation. He made a quick note of what was needed for the rite, then slammed the lid of his laptop shut before the force could grow any stronger.

The feeling of power vanished the instant he was off the site, but it had been enough to persuade him this was the real deal, enough to drive him back into town for supplies. And he felt a kind of savage thrill at that. The idea that a powerful being could be called on to do his bidding and hurt whoever had stolen from him; it filled him with a dark excitement unlike anything he'd felt before. Come nightfall, the thief was going to regret ever crossing Connor Blakesley.

* * *

Dusk couldn't come soon enough. With shaking hands, Connor opened up the laptop to find the page still displaying in his browser. He had another read through the instructions, then placed the candles he'd bought in a circle with an incense cone at its centre, and an offering of raw steak. Striking a match, he went round the circle anti-clockwise, holding it to the wick of each candle till one by one they were all lit. The match nearly fell from his sweaty fingers as he brought it to the incense in the middle, he was trembling that much in giddy anticipation of what might happen. But moments later smoke began to rise and twist through the still air of the flat. Then he started to chant.

"Alal-vargr, hear my call," he intoned. That tingling sensation was back with the uttering of the entity's name, and each of the flames flickered and bowed as if blown by an invisible being. Yet the air remained still and dead as far as he could tell. "Born of darkness, feel it within me and the dark desires driving me this night. I ask of you to lend me your dark power and aid me in bringing vengeance to those that have wronged me. Unleash your wrath on my enemies and carry out revenge in my name, in whatever way you see fit. Maim them, kill them, make them pay with blood. Alal-vargr, I summon thee. Hear my call! Go forth; walk our mortal plane bound only by my will. Let me have my revenge!"

As soon as he fell silent, the world was thrust into darkness, the lights going out with no warning in what anyone else would assume was just a power cut. At the same moment his door flung open, with a cry of "No!"

Only the candles remained burning, holding back just enough shadow to make out the same guy from the club the night before. Connor sneered in the dim light, his eyes glowing red momentarily before fading back to their normal colour. "Too late. It is unleashed."

The stranger backed away. There was no point in killing Connor now. The student had become linked to the hellish being through the summoning, but killing him would only free the thing to slaughter millions. There was nothing more to be done here. Despite his best attempts to stay one step ahead of the thing and prevent it crossing over, he had failed.

There was a time when Shane had considered Josh his brother, but of late he was just another annoyance in a life that had become less than perfect. That night he was being especially irritating, disturbing Shane yet again when he was trying to enjoy the only thing left in his relationship with Chantelle while she was still in the mood. It wasn't like he could ring up the power company and demand they sort things out just so Josh could go back to watching TV.

Shane feigned deafness as Chantelle slid her hand down his

boxers, until Josh's incessant whining turned to screams. The two sat bolt upright, their hearts already pounding in their chests.

"What the fuck?" Shane said to his girlfriend. He shouted out "Josh, you better not be screwing around down there!"

There was no reply.

"Go on, babe, go see what the idiot's up to now."

"OMG, he's your friend!" she said. "Do you really expect me to go down there in the dark when someone might have broken in?"

"I'm not going down like this," he replied, still hard.

"God you're such a wanker!"

She grabbed her new phone, intending to use it as a torch, but it was dead. Without it she was forced to grope her way to the door, and down the stairs. Shane lay back, the initial shock of the scream already turning to frustration at the timing of it. If he had to go down there after them before his lust was sated, someone was gonna pay.

Minutes went by with no sound from downstairs, causing him to shout out again. "Well come on then, Chantelle, what the fuck's going on down there?"

When no one replied he groped his way round the room as his girlfriend had done, cursing the both of them. Each step was slow and uncertain, Shane feeling a vulnerability in the pitch black he wasn't used to, and did not particularly like. Managing the stairs was the worst, but he made it into the living room without falling to his death. It was only once he entered the room that he stumbled over something lying across the floor.

Blindly Shane threw out his hands, catching hold of the wall and steadying himself purely by luck. His hand came away slick and wet.

"What the fuck is this? Josh, Chantelle, I'm gonna kill you two when I find yer. Stop dicking about, yer bastards."

He couldn't remember where he'd left his lighter, so he felt his way to the kitchen and rifled through the drawer where they kept the matches. The carpets squelched with each step he took. He struck a match, the flame sparking to life and revealing the same substance he'd touched in the living room, sprayed all over the walls like some ghoulish artwork. The carpet was sodden with it.

The source of the bloody fountain lay in the corner of the kitchen – the largest piece of what had once been Josh, whose instincts had been right all along. The rest of him lay strewn around, an arm draped over the sink like a rubber glove, legs near the doorway, still twitching as if Josh's mind lived on, willing them to carry the rest of him away from his attacker. His head had been ripped off, jaws still wide open in the scream he'd never been permitted to finish. Shane was in a state of shock as he took all this in. Then the flame crept to the end of the match and began to curl round his fingers, causing him to drop it with a string of more curses. But it had been enough to break the spell the horrific scene had left him in which had seemed to last for minutes, not the seconds it had truly been. The carpet was too wet to catch fire and the darkness rushed back in.

"Chantelle? Where the fuck are you? We need to leave, now!"

Again there was no answer. He felt for one of the larger kitchen knives and lit another match, trying not to look at what had once been his housemate, not out of any grief or feelings of loss, but out of fear that the same would happen to him if he didn't get out of there soon.

The second match burnt out as he re-entered the living room. He lit a third one, expecting to see his girlfriend cowering behind something. If she didn't show herself before he reached the front door he was escaping without her, and the stupid bitch could save herself.

Chantelle was, in fact, lying on the floor, and it was her remains that had caused Shane to stumble on his way into the room. Her death had been quicker than Josh's, though it had been no less brutal. Something had clamped its jaws around her upper body, biting into her chest, its fangs scraping across her throat and severing the vocal cords before she'd even had chance to scream. Her ribs stuck out at odd angles, her once flawless breasts hanging off in bloody tatters, her heart and lungs bitten in two.

Shane backed away, another emotion he was unused to taking hold of his heart and squeezing it so that it pumped at an unhealthy rate, flooding his body with adrenaline. People were supposed to fear him, goddamn it! He was not the victim anymore. People were supposed to fear him now!

The knife gave him just enough confidence to shout out again, though his voice would not come out quite as strong or steady as he tried to make it.

"Whoever you are, yer better show yerself right now. You have no idea who you're fucking with, yer twat!"

Doubt nagged at him as the seconds ticked by with no reply. Could a human really inflict this kind of damage? Both Chantelle and Josh, ripped apart so savagely in the space of what could only have been minutes. It seemed more like the work of a large animal, but what kind of animal could do that to a person? The largest carnivore in the UK had to be the fox, right? And could a fox really do that? He didn't think so.

Shane turned in time to see shadows shift behind him, causing him to swear again and drop another match. He struggled to light a fourth, panicking now. Something was in here with him. It had killed Josh and Chantelle and it was his turn next. All semblance of bravery fled before the rising terror, on a par with that dread he used to feel whenever his father came home stinking of booze, or his mother started on the wine, knowing a beating was sure to follow.

Another flame burst into life in time to see something big and muscular running towards him. His fingers were shaking so badly he promptly dropped it, barely managing to ignite a fifth, the flash of light revealing huge, gaping jaws inches from his face. That match died as fangs closed around his lower jaw, ripping it clean off and leaving his tongue hanging limply. The other two had been granted quick deaths but Shane's fate was to be much crueller.

What had looked to be a huge beast proceeded to ravage its victim, breaking several bones in his body but not severing any major arteries. When it finally retreated the young man was left to suffer a slow and agonising end, alone there in the darkness and too damaged even to scream for help.

And Connor, linked to the entity he had summoned, was able to see it all, playing in his mind like a movie shot through the eyes of the creature, and he revelled in the dark pleasure it brought him. His thoughts, twisted and still driven by anger and the need for revenge, turned to his next target – the girl who had denied him in the club. A name popped into his mind.

"Laura."

The beast heard and loped off into the night, already on the hunt.

* * *

Laura had been out walking when the power cut hit, visiting her sister. She wiped away a tear for her parents, the anniversary of their death being the real reason why she had turned Connor down the previous weekend. Her friends had thought a night out would do her good, but the pain was still too raw to allow any real enjoyment, and she wasn't in the right frame of mind to get back on the dating scene anytime soon.

The darkness was so complete that she used her phone as a torch, pausing as she reached the cemetery where her parents were buried. She was surprised to see the shadowy form of a man knelt by a couple of gravestones, thinking it an odd time to visit. Her own sense of loss caused a feeling of connection that defied logic, even though he was a complete stranger and could be dangerous for all she knew. She felt compelled to call out to him.

"Hey, are you okay in there?" she shouted. When he didn't reply she glanced around nervously, unsure whether they were supposed to be in the graveyard at that time of night, but risked walking over to him.

"Hey, weren't you at the club yesterday?" she tried again. "What are you doing out here at this time; is everything okay?"

"No, I've failed," he answered with such misery, her heart instantly went out to him. "I screwed up and now it's starting again, just as it did back then."

He gestured at the headstones. In the torchlight she could make out the names Johnny and Mary: his grandparents, she assumed, judging from the dates.

"What's your name?"

"John."

"Well, John, whatever it is, I'm sure they'd forgive you. I doubt they'd want you to be out here at any rate; I think it's time we were both safe back in our homes."

He looked so forlorn, kneeling there in the shadows amongst the dead. His head was bowed, perhaps with that sense of failure he'd just expressed as much as grief for his lost loved ones. At first she didn't think he was going to answer, but then he locked gazes with her and she felt like something deep and unspoken passed between them.

"Yeah, I guess you're right," he said, getting to his feet. "But I have nowhere to go now. I don't live round here anymore and I was supposed to be going back today, but I've missed my last train and the place I was staying at is fully booked."

"Well I guess you can crash at mine, if you'd like?"

Laura heard herself speak the words, felt them vibrate along her vocal cords and across her lips, but there had never been a conscious decision to make such an offer. It seemed to her almost as though something had spoken through her, yet again there came that sense of a connection between them and it drove away any fears or doubts she might otherwise have had. Besides, she was too nice to withdraw the invitation once she'd made it.

"That's very kind of you, thank you."

"Come on, then. It's not far. My name's Laura, by the way."

John was quiet on the walk to her flat, but the moment they went inside and she locked the door, he reached round her to pull the security chain across. She backed away from him, startled, but he just stood with his back to it, barring the main exit. Laura stared, though after that initial alarm there came no fear. A part of her continued to wonder what had possessed her to bring a stranger into her home, especially one who was acting so odd. Yet she did not sense any ill intent in his behaviour, unusual though it was.

No, he was looking at her not with the eyes of a madman intent on harming her now there was no escape, but with the concern of a friend, wishing only to protect her from the dangers of the outside world. And there was a power to him that went beyond his muscular form, some kind of inner power that gave her a feeling of safety. It made no more sense than any of the other emotions he'd invoked in her, yet she trusted her instincts. John would not hurt her.

"Okay, now we're back I need you to listen," he said. "Your life is in danger."

"What?"

"Trust me, the thing that stalks you may defy belief, but I assure you it's as real as we are. You're going to have to follow my instructions if you want to live to see the morning."

"Someone's after me? Shouldn't we call the police?"

"Not someone, some *thing*."

That did give rise to fear. It was the way he said it, and the expression of deadly seriousness on his face. The words should have sounded crazy but she could see he believed everything he was saying, and that unnerved her far more than any other signs of insanity he might have given off. She began to back further away, into the lounge.

"Maybe it was a mistake bringing you back here. I think you should leave and let the police handle it."

"The police can't help you now. I don't mean to scare you, but you need to know the truth if you're going to survive the night."

"And what is the truth?" she asked, reaching behind her for something to use as a weapon. Her fingers closed around the table lamp by the sofa.

"Do you know much about Norse mythology? Have you heard the story of the two wolves that chase the sun and the moon, and will one day eat them?"

Laura couldn't help but laugh. Whatever she'd been expecting him to come out with, it wasn't that. "You're telling me I'm being hunted by some mythological Viking wolves?"

"Sköll and Hati, hell hounds, black dogs; they're all myths related to sightings of the same beast. The Vikings were right in that one day he will 'eat' the sun. He's a creature of shadow and darkness, bent only on extinguishing all light, both literal and the metaphorical light we call life. That's where the idea of black dogs and death comes from. Light is his enemy and light is the only way we can keep him at bay."

"How do you know all this?" Her brief feeling of amusement gave way to another bout of unease. John was not laughing. This wasn't a joke to him, a wind-up to play on her emotions in an attempt to seduce her like it might have been for other guys. He truly believed in this thing, whether it was real or not.

"Few have survived encounters with the beast, but the families of those that do are forever touched by shadow. He last walked the Earth in World War Two. The corruption at the heart of mankind will always call to him, and what better breeding grounds for darkness than during a war? But there has to be some kind of ritual to allow him to cross that final veil between realities. I don't know which side was responsible for summoning him, but once he's here, he kills the enemies of whoever he's bound to until he breaks free of that hold and can run wild, killing anything and everything in his wake like a force of pure destruction."

Laura glanced at the window across the room from her, wondering if her instincts had been wrong. Maybe she should make a run for it before he turned violent. John was clearly deranged, but the safest thing seemed to be to play into his fantasies, for now at least. "Touched by shadow?"

"I have the ability to sense when he's close to crossing into our world, which is what brought me back here in the first place. A vision of the boy who summoned him led me to the club last night, and I followed him home. You see, I've made it my duty to put a stop to any potential opportunities which would allow him to take that final step. But something clouded my senses this evening and so tonight I failed in that duty, and now he's here again. The deaths have already begun. He's still bound to the will of his summoner for now, but the connection twists the mind of any would-be masters stupid enough to attempt to enslave him, and they begin to see enemies everywhere. Something you did upset the guy he's bound to, and he's made you the next target."

"Me?"

"My ability also lets me see who his next victim is. It's you, Laura."

"Okay, say I believe you – what do we do now?"

He was about to answer when a spasm seemed to run through him and he fell to his knees, clutching at his chest as if in pain. Laura watched with wide eyes as he ripped open the front of his shirt to reveal blackened flesh bulging beneath his skin, as if his heart had turned necrotic and was struggling to break free of the taint afflicting it. Veins stood out around it, the blackness slowly spreading. Dog tags hung around his neck, relics from a life that seemed aeons ago.

"See, it's real," John grunted through clenched teeth. "His presence calls to the darkness in me."

"I don't understand," she said, starting to back away again. The weight of the lamp in her hand brought little comfort when she seemed to be facing the impossible.

"I'm touched by his darkness. Most of the time it lies dormant but when he's close it begins to awaken and takes a hold of my heart. The closer he is, the more powerful it grows, until it takes me over. We don't have much more time. Grab something to start a fire and when he comes, run! I'll hold him off as long as I can. Find somewhere you can get a real blaze going and keep it burning till morning comes. It's your only hope!"

Her phone died just as a growl sounded from within the room. She froze, well and truly terrified now.

John swore and reached into his jacket for the hand flares he carried. A twist of the cap and pull of the cord brought forth a burst of light, briefly illuminating the room and giving a glimpse of a dark, muscular figure prowling the edges of the artificial glow. He paid it little heed, focusing instead on the girl he felt honour bound to save.

Still on his knees, John struggled over to her, the veins swollen black along most of his torso now. The pain was just as intense as the last time the darkness had sought to take him over, every movement made excruciating by it. Once that black in his veins crept up to his face he would be lost, but he continued to fight his losing battle for her sake, clinging to the lighter side of his nature with all his will.

He won his fight just to reach Laura and dug inside his jacket again, this time retrieving a lighter which he pressed into her empty hand. Giving her a gentle push, he activated a second flare and shouted at her to go, watching with satisfaction as the light pushed back the darkness long enough for her to run to the door and make her escape. He'd known such physical barriers were useless against a thing of shadows, but he'd slid the security chain across in case Connor showed up as well. The odds were already stacked against them without that fool joining the battle.

The second flare died and another surge of pain pushed the corruption closer to his brain. What he hadn't told Laura was the temptation the nearness of the hellish creature awoke in him, the temptation to give in to the darkness and join the hunt. He had the training and the discipline to fight it for now, but he didn't know how long he could hold it off, just as he didn't know how successful he would be at holding off the black taint itself.

John lit another flare, hoping to distract the beast – Alal-vargr – long enough for Laura to find safety by the light of a fire. But that hope was in vain. The shadow creature was already giving chase, and if he caught her in the dark that would be it, her life would be forfeit. John couldn't let that happen. He might have failed to prevent the summoning in the first place, but he could at least fight to save the innocents the beast and his summoner marked for death. So he gritted his teeth and rose back to his feet, limping after the two as fast as his condition would allow.

* * *

Laura managed to reach a nearby field where she knew there was a large haystack. It was quick to catch fire and she stood as close to the blaze as she could, hoping it was bright enough to keep her safe.

By its light, she was able to see the demonic being as he approached, like a patch of darkness that was somehow more complete than the surrounding shadows. At first he appeared as a large and muscular wolf with fur as black as night, more terrifying to behold than any mortal beast. But then the shadows shifted and he became something of a wraith – skeletal and corpse-like with seemingly less substance to him than his other state, as if made up of no more than shadow himself. Yet somehow he was no less impressive for the loss of his muscles. And despite his dark form, his eyes glowed red, the only source of apparent life to this thing that was otherwise a force driven by darkness and destruction.

Still holding her lamp, Laura took aim and flung it with all her might. She could have sworn she'd hit the creature but he didn't even flinch, and the lamp looked to pass through him, smashing where it landed on the hard ground.

Alal-vargr snarled, but he hadn't yet come to full power in the earthly realm. To extinguish their manmade lights was easy, unnatural as they were, but the natural light of the fire was more of a challenge. So he used his other resource, the fool that had sought to bind him. The connection went both ways, and the beast was far more powerful than any human would ever be. He planted the suggestion in the boy's mind that he should come and witness the great power he'd unleashed, then retreated into the darkness and waited.

Connor didn't take long to show. He knew the fire was preventing him from having his revenge on Laura but it was burning too fiercely for him to put out, so he grabbed her, intending to drag her away from its safety. She fought back, kicking and screaming for all she was worth, but his grip remained solid and his strength unbreakable. Inch by inch he pulled her away from the flames, far enough for Alal-vargr to lunge forward, then threw her to the ground.

Before the beast's jaws could latch on to Laura's delicate mortal frame, something else collided with his shadowy form. The force of it knocked him off-balance and he fell into a roll, tangled with his attacker in a ball of writhing limbs and slavering jaws. He came to a stop with his belly to the floor and snarled with frustration.

Rising to his feet once more, he shook his opponent from his great back and twisted round to snap at the one who dared interrupt his kill.

Despite the second creature's now monstrous body, the dog tags around his neck identified him as John. He'd lost his fight to keep his human shape and the darkness had spread throughout his body, not just in his veins now but in the very fibre of his being, twisting it into something closer to its origin – the very beast he'd just engaged in combat.

The werewolf watched that mighty maw bearing down on him for the second time in his long life, and for the briefest of moments he was taken back to the night they'd first crossed paths, all those decades ago. He was back in the woods, alone and clutching his gun as he watched those twin flames of evil rushing towards him. Deep down he knew the bullets wouldn't save him after they'd failed all the others, but he fired anyway, pulling the trigger until the gun clicked empty. Then the beast was on him, and he screamed with the same pain and terror as every other soldier to fall to its jaws. And he would have met the same bloody end as the rest of them that night, had it not been for a stroke of sheer luck so improbable that he felt sure it must have been the hand of fate or divine intervention.

A bolt of lightning struck the tree next to them and the wood burst into flame, blazing with a light strong enough to drive off Alal-vargr and keep him at bay for the remainder of the twilight hours. But in a way Johnny had died that night, for the beast's darkness was in him then and he was no longer the same man who'd gone to war. In fact, he was no longer a man at all.

John returned to the present just as the shadow wolf's jaws were about to close on his throat, no longer a helpless human cowering before a mighty predator but a predator himself now. He rolled away before the other beast could finish what it had started that fateful night in the midst of the war, eliciting another furious snarl from his opponent. And with a speed and agility his human self could never have accomplished, he leapt to his feet.

Alal-vargr lunged again but John stood his ground and they wrestled, Alal-vargr desperately trying to break free and continue the slaughter, while he fought to keep hold of his opponent and prevent him from reaching his target. And as they grappled, jaws snapping and claws slashing, Laura tried to inch back towards the fiery haven of the burning haystack. But Connor wasn't about to let her escape. He kicked her until she lay still, then pinned her down.

John knew that powerful as he was transformed, he couldn't win against the other beast in a fair fight. He allowed the two of them to separate while he still had enough of his humanity about him to work the last flares he'd managed to keep in the remains of his shredded trousers. His hands were still mostly human, despite the black fur and the claws, and he was able to light it, temporarily driving the beast back. Then he turned his attention to the boy, who was still struggling with Laura.

He was barely able to stay in control by this point, his mind clouded by a similar darkness to that which had twisted his body: thirsting for blood and violence, just as Connor's mind was clouded through the link the ritual had given him with the creature. But unlike Connor he fought to use it for good, though all he could really do was channel it towards his enemies. So he focused his rage on the boy threatening the life of she who he'd taken it upon himself to protect; she who reminded him so very much of his own love.

It was over in seconds. Connor was no match for the strength and the fury of the werewolf. Alal-vargr howled in triumph as John ripped out the human's throat in a bloody spray, instantly severing the connection. Now he was free to run wild and rampant.

The realisation of what he'd done was enough to grant John temporary control once more. He brandished his last flare at the thing, making sure it didn't come for them again. Alal-vargr wasn't worried. They'd all served their purpose, freeing him to slaughter as he chose.

John turned back to Laura, only to realise his second mistake. She lay by the fire, bloody furrows along her neck where his claws had shredded her skin in the struggle. It was like watching his beloved Mary dying all over again, when the darkness had taken hold for the first time after he'd returned home from the war and he'd lost control.

He howled in anguish as the screaming started, thousands doomed to meet their end before the sun finally rose once more. Maybe they would banish the beast again before he became too powerful and ended the world, even if it took another nuclear bomb. But by then it would already be too late for the countless souls swallowed by shadow, and the creature could only be chased away for so long.

No matter how bright the light it would always burn out eventually. Even the sun would only last so long, and the shadows would always return. This was a war that couldn't be won, and for so many, time had already run out.

NICK STEAD

A lifelong fan of supernatural horror and fantasy, Nick spends his days prowling the darker side of fiction, often to the scream of heavy metal guitars and the purrs of his feline companions. Werewolves are his speciality but only the monstrous kind – you won't find any tame puppies in this author's works!

Fate set him on the path of the writer at the tender age of 15. The journey has been much longer and harder than his teenage self ever anticipated, but 17 years later he is still forging ahead.

Nick is best known for his Hybrid series. He has also had short stories published in various anthologies, and will soon be releasing his first non-Hybrid novel based on the true story of the Pendle witches.

How to find Nick
   Web: Nick-Stead.co.uk
   Amazon Author Page: author.to/nickstead
   Or follow his Social Media channels below

   facebook.com/officialnickstead
   twitter.com/nick_stead

TUG

"FOUR STRANGERS WAKE IN A PITCH BLACK
ROOM FILLED WITH CORD SWITCHES THEY
DAREN'T PULL."

OWEN TOWNEND

When Dudley woke, he thought he had gone blind. He waved a cold, stiff arm in front of his face but could not detect any motion with his eyes. Nevertheless, he stood up as best he could from the cold floor. He wondered what had happened to his bed. Hearing echoes coming from his slightest breath, he wondered where he was full stop.

"Hello?" he spoke with a scratchy voice.

"Yes!" another voice yelled. He seemed quite a distance away. "I'm Reese. Who are you?"

"Dudley."

"Are you hurt?"

"No." Dudley lightly stretched his arms, running fingers all the way up to each of his shoulders. "I don't think so."

"I know what you mean, Dudley. I think I might have cut my leg a bit but I can't see a damn thing." Reese paused. "Can you feel anything around you?"

Dudley was finally getting used to his immediate surroundings, as sparse as they were. "No. Where are we?"

"I have no idea." Reese muttered this before urgency returned to his voice. "Are you sure you can't feel anything at all?"

"It's just a lot of space."

Reese sighed. "There must be a wall nearby."

Dudley touched the back of his head. At least he wasn't bleeding.

"This place must be huge. Why are we here, Reese?"

"I don't know." Dudley could hear frustration creep into the other man's voice.

"The last thing I remember is climbing into bed," Dudley said.

"I was crashing on a friend's sofa for the night."

"So, this has something to do with sleep?"

"I don't know." Reese all but snapped. He coughed. "I don't know, mate."

Dudley shivered. "I think I'm in a cold spot. Are you cold?"

"There's a bit of breeze, I suppose."

"It's worse than that." Dudley could feel goosepimples on the back of his neck.

Reese huffed. "You could move, you know?"

"Where?"

Before Reese could respond, there was a crash. The whole ground shook. Dudley instinctively reached out in front of him. His fingers brushed against something incredibly thin. A length of string.

"What the shit was that?" Reese asked.

"Sorry," a woman's voice announced. "I rushed over when I heard your voices. Did you say your name was Reese?"

"Yes."

"And you, the other voice, are you Rodney?"

"Dudley."

"Right. Sorry."

"And who are you?" he asked.

"Cheryl. I really should have started with that, shouldn't I? Like you did."

"Wait," Reese said. "You said you rushed over here? Can you see somehow?"

"I followed your voices."

"From how far away?"

"I don't know."

"Did you count your steps?"

"No."

Reese's exasperation echoed across the space.

Dudley still felt the string but he didn't announce it. Instead he turned in the direction that he thought Cheryl was in and asked, "Did you feel a wall as you came over here?"

"No. Sorry."

"Then we must all somehow be in the centre of a massive room."

"You mean like a warehouse?"

"Possibly."

"Well, maybe there is something in here. A light switch."

"I wouldn't explore just yet, Cheryl..."

"Ow!"

Dudley clenched up. He didn't notice his fingers slip around the string until they were pinching it hard. "Are you okay, Cheryl?"

"Yes. Just landed on my knee." She paused. "Hang on. There's a piece of string. You know, it could be a toggle switch! Very low though."

A woman's laugh, distant and to the right. Dudley could hear Cheryl's breathing not too far away on his left side so it had to be someone else entirely. As the throaty chuckle continued, Dudley worked out that this other woman was much lower down, maybe even seated on the floor.

"Who is that?" he asked.

"No-one," the voice replied.

"Seriously?" Reese said. "We've all given our names."

"Sensible. But ultimately pointless."

"How so?"

"Cheryl," the woman said, "that's not a toggle switch."

Cheryl squeaked.

"Then what is it?" Reese asked.

"Something you really shouldn't tug."

Dudley suddenly wanted to let go of his own string but then he didn't know if he would still need it. "Does it pour down cold water or something?"

The woman laughed again. "The opposite. It doesn't bring things down. It takes you up."

"Up?" Reese scoffed. "How can a string drag you up?"

The woman sighed.

"Well," Cheryl replied, "couldn't that be a good thing?"

"Look up. Do you see anything there that looks better than down here?"

"I can't see anything at all."

"I rest my case."

"What happens?" Reese made this sound more like a demand than a question.

"I honestly don't know."

"Then why assume it's a bad thing?"

"Because people disappear."

Something occurred to Dudley: "Screaming?"

"Sometimes."

"Wait," he said. "Let's be logical. If you were unexpectedly pulled up out of the dark, wouldn't you be surprised? And wouldn't that surprise come out as a scream? We don't know if it's really anything to be scared about in the end."

The woman chuckled. "Let's be logical, eh?"

"Also, how can we be certain that every string in here will drag you off? One of these might actually be attached to a light."

"You mean," Reese said, "this could be some kind of sick game? Like Russian Roulette?"

Dudley shrugged even though no one could see him. "Maybe."

"Well," Cheryl spoke up, "it's worth a try. I mean, it might do nothing at all, right? That's what you're saying?"

"It's possible."

"All right then. One little tug."

"Don't do it," the mysterious woman whispered, though there was no panic in her voice at all, just resignation.

There was a distinct click. Everyone was silent for a moment.

"Okay," Cheryl said. "I suppose this one's br-"

Dudley was almost knocked off his feet by a rush of wind and Cheryl's scream. He reached out to her with his other hand but then he didn't know exactly where she was in relation to him. Her outcry rose high up and cut out.

"Shit!" Reese yelled.

"I warned her," her voice replied. "And you."

"What do you mean you warned us?" Reese snapped. "You call that a warning? It doesn't sound like you even care!"

"I do care!" The ferocity of the woman stunned both Reese and Dudley into silence.

Dudley wondered why he still had the string in his hand after everything that had just happened. He convinced himself that it was for a rational explanation. No single piece of string could feasibly pull a whole human body up off of its feet. This had to be something else. But what? He ran his fingers up the length to judge the texture, see how far up it really went.

"How many?" Reese asked. "How many people have you heard tug the string and disappear?"

The woman was silent for a moment. "I've lost count. More than a dozen."

"And you warned them like you warned us?"

"Of course."

"Then why did they do it anyway?"

"Why does anybody do anything after being told not to?"

Reese went quiet.

"Hope," Dudley replied, "and an inability to accept an incredible explanation."

"This guy gets it," the woman said.

"Thank you." He gulped. "Perhaps I'm smart enough not to make the same mistakes."

"Perhaps."

"In that case, could you please tell me your name?"

The woman sighed. "All right. It's Helen."

"Hello, Helen. I take it you were around to hear our names?"

"Yes."

"How long were you there while we fumbled around?" Reese asked.

"I only crawled over when you two first started talking."

"And you chose to remain silent until we found out about these bloody strings? Why didn't you warn us straight away?"

Helen didn't seem to have an answer for this or perhaps she just didn't like talking to Reese. His passive-aggression was beginning to get on Dudley's nerves as well.

Nevertheless, he persevered: "Where were you before you woke up here?"

"In a ditch somewhere."

"Really?"

She let out a mirthless chuckle. "Probably."

"Passed out?"

"Of course."

"Then that settles it: we were obviously abducted in our sleep."

"Either that or this is all some kind of elaborate nightmare."

"Shared by four people?" Reese interrupted.

Helen sighed. "That's why I said elaborate."

"I doubt it," Dudley said. He didn't get it: what was currently in his hand felt like a piece of string, damp possibly because of his sweaty palms. Also, it started high above his reach. He was a tall man.

"It could be a church," he muttered.

"What?" Helen said.

"From the cold spots. This place could be an old church."

"What about a warehouse?"

"It could be that too. It's just...I don't think it is."

Already Dudley could hear Reese's frustration simmering.

"What does any of that matter?" he said. "It's high up. It may have a second floor. People are still disappearing! And we're only now hearing about it!"

"I've told you everything I know," Helen replied.

"Have you now?"

"Yes. Short of grabbing one of these strings myself, I don't know what more there is to tell."

Dudley felt guilty about not telling them about his own string. Still, he hadn't learned anything about it yet and didn't want to alarm them any further. Nevertheless, there was still something playing on his mind: "Did they all have time to scream?"

Helen was silent again.

"For God's sake!" Reese bellowed. "Answer him!"

"Not always," she eventually said.

"She's holding back. You're obviously holding back!"

"I'm not! People grab a string, tug it and disappear. Every single time. Sometimes they scream, sometimes they don't, but they're all gone seconds later. That's all I know!"

"But what about Dudley's theory? One of these might turn the lights on."

"I doubt it."

"But you don't say it's impossible? Because you haven't grabbed a string yourself."

"You seriously expect me to take that risk? After hearing so many people get dragged off?"

"A string can't drag people off!"

"Then how else can you explain it?"

Reese seemed to ignore this. "You mean to say you haven't reached up and felt for this super-strong string yourself?"

"Funnily enough, no!" Dudley detected sudden movement from the place where Helen's voice came. "But, if it will shut you up, I'll see what it feels like!"

"Helen," Dudley spoke, "you really don't need to-"

"Apparently I do, Dudders," she replied. "There: I've found one. Have you, Grease?"

"It's Reese," he snapped back, "and yes."

Dudley began to feel lightheaded. Things were going to go bad very fast.

"Guys," he said. "Please don't-"

"Quiet!" Reese snapped.

"Are we honestly doing this?" Helen asked.

"Apparently so," he said.

Although Dudley obviously couldn't see, he looked away.

"I just need to know, you know?" Reese announced. "Surely you can let go of this string. We can both let go right before anything happens."

"We'll see now, won't we?" Helen's voice was as hard as before and a little colder.

"On the count of three," Reese said. "One...two...three!"

Click. Neither Reese nor Helen made a sound. Dudley couldn't even hear them breathing.

"Guys?" he tried.

"I'm still here," Reese replied. "I let go."

"Helen?"

Further silence.

Reese sighed though this sounded more bored than bereft. "She's gone, Dudley."

Come to think of it, Dudley was sure that he heard something in the gap, the slightest scuff of feet. And wind? Maybe a gasp. They stood awhile in the disturbing silence.

"Then again," Reese spoke slowly, "she did lie before."

"I don't..." A sob rose up through Dudley's body. "I really don't think she would pretend to have disappeared."

"She didn't reveal herself to us before now."

"Not now. Not after everything she said." Dudley felt tears make his eyes sticky. "For God's sake, Reese..."

"Don't put this on me! I didn't pull that string for her!"

"You goaded her..."

"I was angry, okay? She'd been lying!"

"She'd been withholding information! But then she told us..."

Reese went quiet again. "Maybe she wasn't the only one withholding. You seem to be pretty calm, all things considered."

"Can't you hear me?"

"Before now, I mean. You were assessing the situation. This is a bloody insane situation to just calmly assess!"

"I was trying to keep it together!"

All Dudley could now hear was Reese's breathing: nasal and unsteady. It seemed to be getting closer.

"Reese? I get it, okay? You can't see a thing. You're scared."

He heard heavy, scraping footsteps. With the echo, it seemed like they could be coming from any direction.

"Reese? Please don't do anything hasty. You may not believe me but I don't...I don't know a thing." Dudley glanced hopelessly around him. "I'm just trying to survive! Like you!"

He could feel the breath of the other man on his face. As Dudley turned away, Reese's hands wrapped around his arm. Dudley struggled to get free; Reese's hands were huge and their grip painful. When he felt them move up to his throat, Dudley kicked out.

They both fell to the floor. Dudley struggled to get Reese off him but he was incredibly heavy. As he elbowed Reese in the face, the string pulled away from him. Was it tangled or snagged on something? Maybe Reese's wrist?

Finally, it occurred to Dudley: he hadn't let go of the string. It had come all the way down with them. Instinctively he let go. A few seconds later, the weight was lifted from him.

"What?" Reese snarled. "Did you-? You, dirty bastard!"

Dudley still couldn't see what was happening but it seemed that the string was having trouble dragging Reese up into the darkness. Nevertheless, he sounded to be much higher up than before.

"Get me down!" Reese yelled. "Now!"

"I can't!" Dudley replied. "You'll have to cut yourself free! Bite into it!"

Dudley heard Reese bite down. A scream soon followed. "I'm bleeding, you prick!"

"Did you cut the string?"

"No! Just my fucking arm..."

Dudley didn't know what to say except: "Try again!"

If Reese did, it wasn't fast enough. Dudley heard him struggle all the way up to wherever the strings took people. As strong as it seemed to be, it clearly had trouble managing someone of Reese's weight.

"I'm sorry!" Dudley called out but now he probably was just shouting in the dark.

Dudley stumbled back onto his feet. As he did, he felt resistance. He couldn't pull his leg fully forward. In the tussle, something had tangled around his ankle: a new string. This one must have been trailing on the ground right behind him. He hadn't noticed.

"Of course."

Dudley let out a noise: gradual pathetic spluttering, following the distinct snap. He didn't attempt to reach down and pick apart the knot, just let what happened next happen as fast as it possibly could.

At least for a moment, there was a flash.

OWEN TOWNEND

Owen Townend is a Yorkshire-born, Yorkshire-bred writer who is strong in the arm but only due to excessive typing. Once he has cleared the truly terrible puns from his head, he writes short speculative fiction, some of which has been published in books like *Liberty Tales* by Arachne Press, *Circling the County* by the Huddersfield Authors' Circle and The Dinesh Allirajah Prize for Short Fiction 2020 - *AI Stories* by Comma Press.

Owen did his book-learnin' at Sheffield Hallam University and now humbly claims the title of Master Bachelor of All Arts, whatever that even means. In recent years, he's become an avid collector of writing group memberships within the Yorkshire area. He is currently working on his first Western novella but the Stetson keeps getting in the way of his keyboard.

How to find Owen.
  Blog – https://mrpondersome.blogspot.com/
  Or follow him on Social Media.

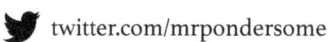 twitter.com/mrpondersome

DELVING

"THREE ADVENTURERS LOOK FOR ANCIENT ARTEFACTS IN A RUINED CITY. WHAT WILL THEY FIND – AND WILL THE GUARDIANS FIND THEM FIRST?"

TIM TAYLOR

Peiku waited by the well at the edge of the village, as Vahe had told him. It was a clear night, but dark. The red hemisphere of Munatu gave a little light, but Nivo, the larger white moon, was nowhere to be seen. He could see nothing, hear nothing. Were the others going to come for him? Part of him would be quite relieved if they didn't.

There was a tap on his shoulder. He jumped, terrified for a moment, then turned to see three fingers in front of his face. He could see no features, just the shadowy figure of a man, silhouetted by the feeble moonlight. Peiku raised three fingers of his own; the man nodded and beckoned for him to follow, setting off without waiting for acknowledgement. The man moved quickly yet silently, and Peiku struggled to keep up. For a moment he thought he had lost contact, but as he reached a line of trees at the edge of the open ground, unseen arms took him and shepherded him into a small hollow.

At first, there was only blackness, then suddenly a pale light illuminated two faces. One was his friend Vahe, grinning from ear to ear.

"Welcome to your first delve, Pei," she whispered. "This is Ravakinu. Ravakinu, meet Peiku."

In contrast to Vahe's, the man's face was stern and intimidating.

"I'm honoured to meet you, sir," said Peiku in a hoarse whisper, unsure how to respond. Then he held up three fingers. The sign was not reciprocated.

"Next time," hissed Ravakinu, "don't stand around by the well, so you're visible to anyone in the village who might be up at night. You *sit* by the well, facing this way, so nobody but us can see you. Or there won't be a next time. Is that understood?"

Peiku nodded and mumbled an apology.

"Right, these are the rules," continued Ravakinu. "Learn them by heart. You do exactly what I tell you. You don't make a noise or speak unless you absolutely have to – and if you do, you speak in a whisper. You don't dig or look for artefacts unless I tell you to, and whatever you find you give to me. If you see or hear any sign of Guardians or other people, you let me know straight away – preferably without speaking. And afterwards – this is very important – you don't say a word to anybody about what you were doing, where you were doing it, or who you were doing it with. Any questions?"

"The light. How do you make the light?" There was no flame – the light seemed to be coming directly from Ravakinu's hand. How was that possible?

"It's an artefact." He opened his hand to reveal a small cylinder, one end of which was emitting the strange light. "I found it a couple of years ago. You can sell them for quite a bit, but I wanted this one for myself. Much better than a flame, for delving."

The light disappeared. "We can't use it when we're on the move – the Guardians would see it half a kilometre away. You need to accustom your eyes to the dark again."

They waited in silence for a minute or two, until Peiku could once more pick out the faint shapes of the trees around them. Then Ravakinu rose to his feet.

"Follow me."

They left the hollow and emerged from the trees onto a track, which led away between two fields of tall ripe godplant, awaiting harvest for the next Homage. The rough gravel of the track crunched underfoot, but Ravakinu gestured for them to slow down and make no noise. Peiku was glad of the silence, for a few minutes later he noticed the faint sound of talking, far behind them. He tapped Ravakinu on the arm and mouthed the word 'voices'.

"Into the field, now!" hissed Ravakinu. "And don't make a noise."

They eased their way between the thick, rubbery stems as delicately as they could, then crouched down. The voices grew louder – soon the Guardians would be upon them! Peiku held his breath and tried to be motionless, but there was nothing he could do about the pounding of his heart. Surely it must give him away.

He could hear two distinct voices. They seemed youthful, excited, and soon he could make out words: "..., going to find ...", "... where we can sell it ..." as two vague shapes became visible through the foliage, and the tramp of their feet approached, then faded away. Peiku released a sigh of relief. These were clearly delvers too.

"Idiots!" said Ravakinu once the two walkers had passed. "They're going to get caught, blundering about like that. Schoolchildren out for adventure, without a clue what they're doing."

"Should we warn them?" asked Vahe.

"No. I don't want anything to do with them. Best leave them to it. With any luck they'll draw the Guardians' attention away from us."

They waited a few minutes, to leave some distance between themselves and the other delvers, then returned to the track once more.

They walked on in silence until the godplant fields were behind them and the track petered out in an area of broken waste ground. Ravakinu turned to face Peiku and Vahe, then pointed off to the right. Peiku followed him as best he could, but in the darkness he stumbled two or three times on stones, prompting hisses of censure from their leader.

At last, they reached a tall wooden fence. It was twice the height of a man: Peiku wondered how they were going to get over it. But Ravakinu showed no inclination to do so, instead slowly following the fence to the left. At length they came upon a large bush. Ravakinu crouched down and motioned for the others to do so as well. The pale light illuminated his face once again.

"This is where we cross," he whispered. "We can get under the fence here. Any second thoughts? It's not too late to go back. If you get caught out here, it's a breach of curfew and a slap on the wrist. Beyond the fence is forbidden ground. Get caught there and you are in major trouble. The Guardians are within their rights to execute anybody they find delving in the Old City, and sometimes they do. People I knew have died there."

He looked pointedly at Peiku. "Still sure you want to go in?"

Peiku was not sure at all, but when he looked over at Vahe, her face had an uncharacteristic expression of grim determination. He couldn't back out now.

"I'm sure."

"Right. Those rules I told you to learn by heart. What are they?"

"Ummm ... Don't make a noise. Do what you tell me and don't do any delving unless you say so. Give whatever we find to you. And don't talk to anybody afterwards."

"Good enough. You forgot the one about letting me know if you see or hear any other people, but you did that earlier, so I'll let you off. You break any of those rules inside the fence, even once, and you're on your own. I will not take you back to the fence – I will have nothing to do with you. Understood?"

"Understood."

"Okay." He pulled aside some foliage to reveal a small space under the fence. It hardly seemed big enough to get through. "I'll go first and make sure the coast is clear. Peiku, wait a few seconds and then follow me. Vahe, you go last and do a final check that we're not being followed."

He turned to Peiku. "You go through feet first. It's tight, but you're skinnier than me so you should be okay. Watch me.

There's another bush on the other side, so it's a bit tricky getting out, but I'll help you."

Ravakinu lay on the ground and put his feet through the hole. First pushing with his hands against the earth and then pulling upon the planks of the fence itself, he eased himself through. There was a rustle of branches on the far side, then silence. Peiku looked at Vahe. She nodded. He lay down and tried to copy what Ravakinu had done. He put his feet through the hole and found that his legs slipped through easily enough as he pushed against the ground. He could feel branches on the other side. Now his hips were beneath the fence and his body was hard against the ground. He pushed again and moved another few centimetres. But his clothing was snagged – he was stuck!

He fumbled with the cloth, trying to pull it free, but that seemed to make things worse. Remembering what Ravakinu had done, he grabbed the bottom of the fence and tried to lever himself through, but to no avail. The hard wood was pressing down on his chest, biting into his ribs with every breath. He was trapped! The urge to cry out was almost overwhelming, but he fought it down.

"I'm stuck!" he whispered to Vahe. She too tried to free his clothes and push him through, but with no more success. He began to wonder if he was going to remain here, to be found by the Guardians in the morning.

He felt his legs being enveloped in a tight grip. Then, with a sudden jerk and a sharp tearing sound, he was free. Now he could pull on the planks to get the rest of his torso and head through the gap. Relieved and dishevelled, he dusted himself off on the far side. Barely had he regained his composure when Vahe – more lithe and slender than either of the males – slid under the fence without trouble. She grinned and handed him an object. His trowel – brought along in the expectation of using it to dig. It had been inside his jacket, now ripped open.

"I think this was your problem," whispered Vahe. She was probably right. A lesson to be learned.

Ravakinu tapped them both on the shoulder and beckoned for them to follow. He was much more circumspect now than he had been outside the fence, creeping forward just a few steps at a time before pausing to look and listen for any sign of trouble. After they had proceeded in this way for a few dozen metres, Peiku began to see the remains of what had once been walls all around them, protruding only a few centimetres from the ground. Ahead, though, were some more substantial ruins, dimly visible as darker shadows against the near-black sky.

As they drew closer, Peiku could now see an irregular wall of almost waist height on their right. They followed the line of this until it turned at right angles, blocking their path, but they were able to clamber through a breach in the wall without difficulty. They found themselves in what appeared to be a broad street between two rows of ruined buildings. Those on the other side seemed taller than the ones they had seen so far – their looming bulk blocked out much of the sky.

Ravakinu scanned the street in both directions, then motioned for the others to follow him across. As they did so, the shapes of the old buildings became clearer. Their walls, in places collapsed into mounds of rubble, elsewhere might rise four or five metres to their ragged tops. Here and there, windows and doorways could be seen. Ravakinu was leading them straight towards one of the doorways. He paused as they reached it, listened, and then went in. Peiku felt his heart pumping faster as he followed Vahe over the threshold – *I am inside one of the buildings of the Ancients!*

It was noticeably darker inside. Though the building had no roof, Munatu was out of sight, hidden behind a wall, and they had only starlight to see by. Peiku, feeling his way along a wall, lost sight of the others entirely and was forced to whisper, "I can't see you – it's too dark."

"I'm here," whispered Vahe, just a few steps ahead. Ravakinu, a similar distance in front of her, returned to speak to them both.

"I can't use the light maker in here, where it might be seen from the street – there are always Guardians patrolling the Old City. But we will need it if we are going to delve. What I am looking for is an interior room, surrounded by others, so the light will be contained. This one is no good – windows in every wall. If you can't see to follow me, you'd better stay here till I've found a suitable place. You two go and sit in the corner nearest the doorway we came in by, and I'll come and get you. Don't move, and stick to the Rules – don't start chattering away like those idiots we saw earlier."

They all returned to the doorway, made visible by the pale moonlight beyond it. Vahe and Peiku felt their way along the wall to the corner and Ravakinu left, with the briefest of waves.

In the corner, with their backs against the cold damp wall, it was not only dark but completely silent. Time had passed quickly while they were making their way to the old city. Now Peiku found himself counting the seconds and minutes away.

"D'you think it'll take him long to find somewhere?" he whispered.

"I hope not. I don't like it here."

"Me neither. I hope the Guardians don't find him before he gets back."

"I just hope they don't find *us*."

There was a tremor in Vahe's voice that Peiku had never heard before. She had always seemed completely fearless. He reached out for her hand. She took it and squeezed like a drowning man clutching a lifeline.

After a while, Peiku could make out the sound of footsteps in the old street beyond the doorway. At first, he thought it was Ravakinu, but then there were voices – not the excited chatter that he had heard earlier, but deeper, more purposeful. His hand closed around Vahe's like a vice.

"Guardians!" he whispered in her ear.

Sure enough, as the footsteps drew closer, he could begin to make out words.

"They came in this direction. I reckon they'll be hiding out in one of these old buildings."

The footsteps stopped. Peiku could see some kind of flickering light beyond the door – white, like that from Ravakinu's artefact; not the yellow light of a burning torch. Then a strange bright circle appeared on the far wall of the ruined building and hung there for a moment like the disc of some weird moon. It began to sweep to and fro across the room. Peiku could see a booted foot in the doorway. He huddled into the wall, not daring even to breathe, and felt Vahe bury her head in his shoulder. Now the white disc was coming towards them!

"You're wasting your time," said a different voice. "They were just kids. They'll have scarpered by now. Run home to their mummies."

"I suppose you're right."

As quickly as it had arrived, the white disc was gone. The footsteps resumed, and gradually faded away. Peiku let out a long gasp.

"Thank the God for that!"

Vahe threw her arms around him and Peiku hugged her back. Suddenly he no longer felt afraid but exhilarated. This was living for real, not the bland existence of home.

"I thought we were done for," whispered Vahe.

"Me too. Whatever happens now, I'm always going to remember this night."

As the pair continued their excited whispering, they failed to hear the approach of another set of footsteps until a figure strode through the doorway and they were both illuminated by a cone of white light.

"I thought you two were supposed to be keeping quiet. Think yourselves lucky it's me and not those two who went past just now. I've been following them, and they've been looking for those noisy fools we met earlier on. The Guardians are out of sight now; we should be okay, for a while at least. Follow me."

They returned to the street and followed Ravakinu to a junction where another street joined from the right. Down there were more shells of buildings. Ravakinu entered one that seemed significantly bigger than the ruins they had seen before, though no less derelict. They followed him inside, through a second doorway that was just visible on the far side of the large room and then a third beyond that.

In here it was completely dark, until the light from Ravakinu's artefact suddenly illuminated the room. It was small – about three metres by four – and apart from the doorway there were no openings in the walls, which were almost complete, rising two and a half metres to where the ceiling would once have been. Ravakinu placed the device on a ledge in a corner, from which it cast a pale light over the whole room.

"From the lack of windows, I'm guessing this was once a storeroom. That makes it a more promising site than most for finding things – though we're probably not the first delvers to have that thought. We'll spend two hours here and then we'll make our way back, so we can be sure everyone will be home well before it starts to get light. I want one person keeping a lookout at all times – you never know when those Guardians may come back this way. Vahe, you take the first shift while I show this lad how to dig."

When Vahe had left, Ravakinu took Peiku to the far side of the room and crouched down.

"Right, the way we do this is to go through a room in strips, about a metre wide. When it's covered in grass, we start by taking the turf off in cubes, like this ...." With his trowel, he cut around a square of about 20cm, then, by levering the blade underneath, lifted the whole piece bodily from the earth and put it to one side.

"We'll do that for the whole of the first strip, keeping all the turves together in a pile. That way, we can put them back when we've finished. See, you never finish delving a whole room in a single night. If we find anything, we might want to come back for more, but we don't want the Guardians to see we've been digging or they might set a trap for us. Then, when we've taken the top off the first strip, we dig out the soil, bit by bit, looking for anything that might be worth keeping. And we put the soil in another pile, so we can shovel it all back in the hole when we've finished. Right then, have a go at cutting a square of turf."

Peiku copied what Ravakinu had done and found that he was able to remove the square without too much difficulty. He put it next to the one Ravakinu had cut.

"Not bad. Okay then, let's clear this strip. You carry on from that end and I'll start at the other. If you see anything when you've taken off the top, let me know."

Peiku began to cut out squares of turf as he had been told. It was not quite the exciting work he had thought delving would be, but he found a quiet satisfaction in it. Underneath the turf was a thin, dusty soil, dotted here and there with fragments of a strange white stone. He picked one up – two of its sides were straight and smooth, and at right angles to each other – not like any pebble he had ever seen.

"It's concrete," said Ravakinu. "The artificial stone the ancients made their buildings with."

After a while, a metre-wide strip was clear and two piles of turves sat by the walls of the room.

"Good. Now we sift. Work your way down the strip, just like you did with the turf. Take off about three centimetres of soil at a time and start a pile near the strip. But leave yourself room to get out quickly if you need to. You do it like this." Ravakinu took a trowelful of soil and flicked through it with his fingers before pouring it onto the pile. Then another, and another.

"Clear enough? All right. I'll take a shift on lookout now. You and Vahe work from opposite sides. Take off the top few centimetres all the way down the strip. We do it in layers, rather than going all the way down in one go – it could be over a metre before we get down to the concrete base. And if you find anything interesting, come and get me."

Ravakinu left, and a few seconds later, Vahe joined Peiku in the room. She seemed relieved to be out of the shadows.

"Isn't this amazing? You and me in an ancient building, digging for buried treasure!"

"Amazing," agreed Peiku. The ground didn't give any appearance of being full of treasure, but this was a storeroom, Ravakinu had said. Who knew what might still be here?

They set to work, methodically sifting the soil from both ends of the strip towards the middle. Each time he lifted the trowel, Peiku felt a little surge of hope that it would contain something ancient, but time after time there was only soil, pieces of concrete and the occasional worm. The pile grew as he shuffled bit by bit towards the centre of the room. Emptying his trowel one more time onto the pile, he moved along, only to bump into Vahe, who was coming in the other direction. They laughed.

"Found anything?" she asked.

"Some bits of concrete. And lots and lots of soil."

"I guess we just have to be patient. If there is anything here, it's probably buried much deeper."

"So, we start again and do another layer." She smiled and nodded.

As time went on, Peiku worked faster, no longer giving each trowelful of soil more than a cursory glance. If something was worth finding, it would be easy enough to see, wouldn't it? They finished the second layer markedly quicker than the first, and started again.

About half a metre into the third layer, Peiku's trowel struck something. He dug some soil away from the obstruction and saw a line of dark grey material protruding from the ground. It didn't look very exciting, but it was straight – surely that meant it was manmade?

"Vahe, I think I've found something."

She came to look over his shoulder as he dug, first on one side of the object and then on the other, then tried to pull it out. It didn't want to budge, but after a little more digging, he was able to pull it from the soil. It was rectangular, roughly fifteen by thirty centimetres, jagged at one end where it must have been broken at some point, and about two centimetres thick. It was hard and smooth like metal, but very light and not cold to the touch. As he brushed the soil off it with his hand, some symbols became visible, like the symbols that could be seen on ancient buildings. There could be no doubt.

"You've found an artefact! On your first ever delving trip. You lucky devil! I've been three times and I've never found anything."

They hugged each other and did a little dance of delight.

The figure of Ravakinu loomed in the doorway, hands on hips.

"What the hell is going on in here? How many times do I have to tell you? Don't make a noise!"

"I'm sorry, Ravakinu. We were excited because Peiku has found an artefact."

"Really? Let me have a look."

Peiku handed over what they had found. Ravakinu took from his pocket a circle of curved glass, and began to examine the object with it.

"Well, it's ancient all right, but it's not really an artefact – just a panel or something that's broken off a bigger object – a piece of furniture, maybe. I don't think there's any technology in it."

"Technology?"

"What the priests call 'sorcery'. The ancients knew how to make objects *do* things, just like my artefact gives out light. This thing doesn't do anything, it's just a broken piece of ancient stuff. It's not worth any money. Here. You can keep it as a souvenir of your first delve if you want. It's no use to me. Just make sure you hide it somewhere nobody but you is going to find it."

He handed the object back to Peiku.

"You might as well do your shift outside now. I'll take over in here with Vahe."

As Peiku left the room, his eyes needed time to adjust and at first he could see nothing at all. The dimmest of rectangular shapes slowly emerged from the blackness – the door to the large space through which they had entered the ruined building. He walked cautiously towards and then through it. The larger room had several windows, through which he could see the street beyond.

There was a flickering light, like the one that had almost found him and Vahe earlier on. He rushed straight back to the room.

"Guardians!" he hissed. Immediately, the room went dark.

"Don't try to pick anything up," whispered Ravakinu. "Don't make a sound, and be ready to run."

The sound of voices told them that the Guardians had

entered the building. Peiku recognised them as the two who had nearly caught them before.

"I definitely heard something in this direction."

"Probably nothing – I didn't hear it."

"All the same, I'm going to search this place. It looks like just the sort of building where you might find delvers."

Ravakinu tapped the others on the shoulder and whispered. "Let's make our way towards the back of the building. We don't want to get trapped in here. But slowly and silently."

As the Guardians began to search the outer room, the three delvers crept in the opposite direction. There was no light to see by, so they had to feel their way along the wall. Peiku could hear the heavy footsteps of the Guardians coming closer. He wanted to melt into the wall and disappear.

In the pitch blackness, Ravakinu stumbled on a rock and let out a stifled cry.

"Delvers - get them!"

"Run!" Just for a moment, Ravakinu's light revealed a doorway in the far wall, then all was black again.

Peiku could see nothing, but ran in the direction of the doorway. His shoulder made painful contact with the edge of the wall, but he was through. Which way now? A hand took his and dragged him to the left. Another doorway was just visible a few metres ahead. They ran for it, heedless of whatever rocks or stumps might be there to trip them up. As they passed through, he could hear the shouts of the Guardians behind. Then there was a flash and a deafening bang. And another, and another.

"Fire sticks! Those things can kill you."

It was Vahe's voice and, as they emerged onto a street, he could dimly see the outline of her face. They ran down the street, turned right when it joined a larger one and sprinted as fast as their legs would carry them. At last, able to run no more, they stopped at a crossroads and collapsed to the ground, gasping for breath and dripping with sweat. They could no longer hear the voices of the Guardians. There was still the occasional bang of a fire stick, but they seemed far away.

"Sounds like they're still hunting Ravakinu," said Peiku, recovering his breath. "I hope they don't catch him!"

"Oh, he'll be all right. Old bugger's made of cast iron."

For reasons he didn't understand, Peiku suddenly burst out laughing. Vahe did the same, and the two threw their arms around each other in relief. Then, as they relaxed their grip, Vahe put her hands to his head and kissed him on the lips. Though Peiku was taken by surprise, he did not pull away but gave himself to the kiss, allowing it to engulf him. Only when they finally separated did he think about what they had done.

"We shouldn't be doing this. It is forbidden. The Code ..."

Vahe laughed. "You're inside the Old City after dark, running away from the Guardians and carrying an illegal ancient artefact. And you're worrying about the *Code!*"

Peiku laughed too. She was right, of course – how absurd it was. Once the ultimate rule is broken, all other rules cease to exist. He put his fingers to her cheek – how soft it was! – and kissed her again.

The sharp crack of a fire stick broke the silence. Then another – this time, splinters of concrete exploded from the wall above their heads.

"Run!"

They sprang to their feet and ran for the shelter of the nearest doorway. There was a third bang, and a fourth. They reached the opening and Peiku ran inside, but Vahe fell through the doorway as if she had tripped on a stone.

"Get up, Va, we need to get out of here."

But Vahe was not moving. In the moonlight he could see a liquid glistening on her back. She lifted her head weakly.

"Run, Pei, it's too late for me." She could barely manage to mouth the words. He took her hand, but it was limp and unresponsive. Her head dropped and lay still.

"They've gone into that building. Get them!" The shouts of the Guardians didn't seem far away now.

"Get up, Vahe, please!"

She did not move. With a cry of anguish, Peiku let go of her hand and left her. At the far side of the building a wall had collapsed, allowing him to dash through into a courtyard beyond and vault over another wall into a street. He went down it a little way, then turned into another cluster of ruined buildings. Behind him he could hear the Guardians shouting to each other, trying to work out which way he had gone. He went from one wrecked building to another, putting as many walls as he could between him and those lethal fire sticks. The voices seemed to be getting steadily quieter. Perhaps they had gone the wrong way? He stumbled through another broken wall, into a street which seemed to lead away from the sound. He took a deep breath and began to run.

At last Peiku could see the perimeter fence a few yards ahead. He had no idea where he had entered, but he knew there was a bush just inside the fence at that point, so he crept slowly along until he found it, throwing himself to the ground whenever he heard voices or saw those strange pale lights flickering in the distance. To his great relief, this time he was able to ease himself through the hole without too much difficulty.

He tiptoed back the way they had come, trying to make no sound. But there were now the beginnings of a faint light in the sky, and the path lay clear in front of him. The slow walk turned into a fast walk, and then into a run. He did not stop until he was back in the village. Only then did fear give way to grief and anger. They killed Vahe! For what? Just for being where she wasn't supposed to be. What harm had she done anybody? He had always disliked the Guardians. Now he hated them.

Later that day, in the privacy of his room and with the full light of the sun streaming through his window, he examined the object he had brought back from the Old City. In the brighter light, he could see not only the large symbols that had been visible when he found it, but also some smaller and fainter ones, arranged below them in a grid pattern. He touched a number of them speculatively, hoping something would happen. Nothing did. It was no artefact, Ravakinu had said – it did not *do* anything. This is what Vahe died for, he thought – this useless piece of ancient junk. He threw it on the floor in disgust.

With a faint click, a small hemispherical protrusion formed on the upper surface of the object. Peiku thought nothing of it – just damage from the impact, he assumed. But a few seconds later, needle-thin lines of red, blue and green light emerged from it and began to rotate, forming swirling patterns of shifting colours. From the swirls there emerged the image of a woman, dressed in strange clothes and smiling, seemingly at him. Then the woman began to speak, in a language he did not understand. Symbols appeared beside her, coming and going as she talked. Peiku drew the curtain, and now the woman seemed real and solid; the symbols were like carved objects hanging in the air. There were images too, which must have been too faint to see before, of tall gleaming buildings and strange devices – the Old City in its glory! How could all this be here, in his small room? He reached out to touch one of the symbols, but his hand passed through it as if it wasn't there.

"Talk to me in my own language," he pleaded. The woman made no response and, after a few more seconds, became silent. She gave a final smile and nod, then vanished.

Peiku picked up the object. The protuberance had disappeared, but the symbols were still there. He pressed them one after the other, but nothing happened. He tried a different order – again, nothing.

He heard footsteps and voices. His family were back from the fields. This would have to wait. He took a last lingering look at his prize before returning it to the hiding place behind his bed.

So Vahe did not quite die for nothing. If only she had lived to see the true nature of what they had found. Peiku had always been reluctant to go delving. He had given in to Vahe's cajoling because he wanted to please her, to spend time with her. Now he knew what drove her to do it, and he owed it to her to carry on.

* * *

Three weeks later, when Munatu was once again alone in the night sky, Peiku felt a tap on his shoulder as he was getting some water from the well. He turned around – it was Ravakinu.

"You interested in a delve tomorrow night? I seem to be short of an assistant."

Is that all you've got to say, thought Peiku. Is that all she was to you, you cold bastard? The words began to form themselves on his lips, but he did not say them. Instead, he thought for a few moments and waited for the anger to subside.

"All right," he said.

TIM TAYLOR

Tim (T. E.) Taylor grew up near Leek in Staffordshire and now lives in Meltham, West Yorkshire, at the opposite end of the Peak District, with his wife Rosa and 14 guitars. Having previously been a civil servant, he now divides his time between creative writing, academic research and teaching Ethics part-time at Leeds University.

Tim's first two novels: *Zeus of Ithome*, which retells the real-life struggle of the ancient Messenian People to free themselves from Sparta; and *Revolution Day*, about an ageing dictator clinging on to power, were published by Crooked Cat. His first poetry collection, *Sea Without a Shore*, was published in 2019 by Maytree Press. Tim is currently working on a science fiction project.

How to find Tim.

Website: https://www.tetaylor.co.uk/
Blog: https://timwordsblog.wordpress.com/
Or follow his Social Media channels below

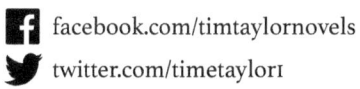

facebook.com/timtaylornovels
twitter.com/timetaylor1

THE FROZEN WASTELAND

"WHEN A RESEARCH TEAM WORKING IN
THE SOUTH POLE MYSTERIOUSLY
DISAPPEARS A PROFESSIONAL MONSTER
HUNTER IS SENT IN."

AQIB ALI

The icy wind rushed across Major John Reins' insulated face as he leaped off the MV-22 Osprey. His combat boots penetrated the fluffy blanket of soft snow which covered the glistening ground as far as the eye could see. The comfortable warmth of the humming helicopter rapidly faded as the harsh sub-zero gusts of the South Pole welcomed his arrival. He double-checked his pistol and battle rifle before proceeding to check his specially adapted combat armour via his standard issue wrist-mounted PDA. He was on his own now.

His headset crackled. "Reins, do you copy? Over." A deep voice growled in his ears.

"This is Reins; I can hear you but the line's not too good. Over," he replied, crouching into the snow to get out of the wind as it danced through the dry atmosphere. "The suit mods are stable though."

"Good. Sorry about the comms, I can't do anything about that; you'll have to bear with it for now. It's the best we can do at the moment due to your secluded location," Colonel Hanson said. Reins could hear the tell-tale clatter of a keyboard in the background.

"So, have you sent me here to freeze my balls off or something? Think I'm a bit rusty after pushing pencils in the office for a month?" Reins grinned.

"Not happy with the promotion?" Hanson teased. "Sending the details through now..."

A notification popped up on Reins' PDA. It marked his objective one mile south of his current location beside a small mountain range. "Could've dropped me off closer."

"The mission required the talents of a high-ranked ranger. Besides, you know we can't risk our expensive equipment getting damaged. Any idea how much one of those choppers costs?" Hanson replied. His tone became more serious. "You should have received the co-ordinates of a top-secret British research station.

The British authorities have tasked us with investigating what happened to their staff who went dark a few days ago. They didn't give me much information except that they were conducting geological surveys in the nearby cave system. Keep your guard up. Your mission is to make your way there by foot, examine the area and relay back what you find. Is that understood?"

"Yes, sir," Reins confirmed. "But we both know 'Geological surveys' is a load of bullshit. I bet they were fucking around with something they shouldn't have been. They always like to call us to clean up their mess once it's too late; never before people start dying."

Reins got up from the clutches of the snow and activated his heads-up display to show his vitals and a small map, along with a digital compass. It had been implemented into his visor as part of the mark-2 Arctic battle suit upgrades.

"I understand your concern but please keep your mouth shut. This is a top-secret operation and we're under non-disclosure. You're the only one with the skills to complete this mission on your own."

"Copy that, sir. Will keep you updated once I get there. Reins out."

Reins mowed through the foot-deep snow towards the lonely research station. He glanced at the diagram of his suit in the corner of his visor: power at ninety-eight percent. It was enough to give him twelve hours of heat through pads covering various parts of his body. He knew he had to use them sparingly if he was to survive in this hellish cold.

Over an hour had passed before the perimeter of the station appeared in his sights. There was no sign of anyone. Research equipment littered the ground, almost completely covered with the dazzling white powder. It seemed he was a few days late to the events that had transpired here. There was no sound except the echoes of the wind as it rushed around his helmet, rocking him like a ship on the ocean. He tapped a button on his PDA, activating the POV camera mounted at the top of his helmet, and called his commanding officer.

"Can you hear me?" Reins asked, scanning the area.

"Affirmative. What's the situation?"

"I'm in the perimeter of the research station; no signs of life. The generators are off. And it looks like they had one hell of a party," Reins replied. In the distance he noticed what appeared to be a fire-blackened outbuilding. "Wait a second, just seen something." He crept towards it, aiming his rifle forward in case something jumped out at him. "There's a shed here." He opened a small vent on his helmet in front of his nose. "Strong smell of burnt diesel. Also burnt snowmobiles. Looks like they emptied all their diesel into the fire. Might be a problem later on when I have to scan the computers."

"Right, I don't see a reason for them to burn all their fuel supplies and their means of escape," Hanson said. He paused. "Could be mind-control...again."

"And you know what that means: demons. I hate demons." He turned away. The memory of the Redhill incident was still fresh in his mind. He could still see the scattered organs and the twitching limbs. And the blood. So much blood. He shook the thought away and looked around.

"I know you hate them but we need to know for sure this is a demon we're dealing with. We're relying on you, Reins."

Reins searched the snow for a trail of footprints, but found none. The heavy snow of the night before must have buried them, but it was always worth checking.

"Still no signs of any movement. Permission to find an entrance, break in and warm my balls up before they fall off."

"Please, Reins, at least try to make contact before you start doing silly things like that." Hanson laughed. "Make your way to the entrance and find the intercom."

"I highly doubt the intercom's going to work without power." Reins replied, walking towards a large bulkhead door. He pushed a small button on the intercom; nothing but a deafening silence filled the speaker. "Yep. Looks like no one's home. Am going in." It took him a moment to pick the lock and push the door open. It was dark as hell in there. Setting his jaw, he entered the silent station.

"You could have waited a bit longer," Hanson said, cursing under his breath.

"Sir, the shit I've been holding in for the last hour is about to end up in my battle suit and there was no way I was going to do it out there," Reins said, switching on the LED light strips around his suit. They revealed the trashed contents of the room. "Where is the goddamn toilet?"

"It's not like I designed the station, you goof. Go look for it. I told you not to eat that spicy curry last night. I'm certainly not going to watch you take a shit. Please don't get yourself killed in the process." Reins heard Hanson chuckle, a door open and close, and then more silence.

The soft helmet light eventually illuminated his objective. Reins hurried through the door of the lavatory and quickly stripped out of his battle suit. He lowered himself onto the ice-cold seat, pistol in hand. The frostbite that his ass would suffer as a result was more than worth the benefit of clear bowels.

Over the headset, he heard someone knocking on a door before a familiar female voice called out. "Colonel Hanson, I have that report you were... Sir, are you..." There was a rustle of paper and approaching footsteps.

"For fuck's sake, don't look at the screen!" Reins shouted.

"Wait... what? Err... John?" the woman stuttered in a

moment of confusion. "No way! You're not doing what I think you're doing?"

"Laura...you shouldn't be watching me. This is a top-secret mission."

"Top secret? As if. You're broadcasting yourself taking a shit. Switch the feed off, you idiot! No wonder the Colonel's gone for a walk. I can't believe they promoted you to Major before me, you absolute wanker!" The loud thud of a door indicated that she had left the Colonel's office.

"Damn," Reins muttered and quickly finished his task. He put his battle suit back on, reconnecting everything.

"Reins?" Hanson called out.

"Sir?"

"You didn't just broadcast yourself taking a shit, did you?"

"I kind of forgot to turn it off," Reins replied with a shrug.

Hanson nearly laughed himself to an early grave. "You absolute numbskull. The entire freaking place is cracking up right now."

"I mean, you did leave the window open on your screen when it's supposed to be a top-secret mission."

"All right *Major Turd*, just carry on with the damn mission. And please, next time turn the damn feed off when you're on the toilet. Get yourself to the security office. There might be some clues as to what's going on in the daily... logs." Hanson chuckled.

"Ha-ha. Let me look around."

Reins finished working his way through the station. Almost all the doors were electronically shut, except for shared areas. Not that this was entirely unexpected. The security he was seeing was standard for this type of station, though it was still frustrating to find himself locked out at every turn. If only someone had left their ID card lying around for him to use. *But at least the restroom wasn't locked,* he thought to himself with a wry grin.

"It's no good, Colonel, I can't get into most of these rooms. Going to need to bring the power back online and someone to do a bit of hacking." Reins sighed at that. He'd tried hacking a similar system once before, with disastrous results. But the earful he'd received from Hanson had been worse.

"Okay, get the power back online but don't mess around with anything! I'll get engineering to hack it. We don't want a repeat of last time."

Reins backtracked all the way to the charred shed. "Hanson, it looks like we may have an issue. I need to get the generators turned on to activate the base but remember all the fuel's been burnt."

"Give the area a good search. Resupply is currently not an option until we know exactly what's going on. On stations like this the fuel is never kept with the vehicles as it is prone to gelling. There must be a storage shed connected to the inside of the station."

"Yeah but everything's locked on the inside."

"The shed has an opening to the outside with a standard lock in the event of a power failure." Hanson sighed. "Sometimes I wonder how you even got promoted to the rank of Major."

Reins searched the back of the building and soon found a wooden door. The padlock was frozen solid; there was no way his lockpick would make it inside. From a small compartment in his suit he produced an old flip lighter, one he had taken with him on every mission. It had saved his life on more than one occasion. He warmed the lock until all the ice had melted and dried out, and then let it cool down before picking it.

There wasn't much to see inside the shed, other than a couple of empty jerry cans and a pile of junk. Reins was about to report this back to Hanson when a small, older-looking can caught his eye from deep within the pile. He twisted the lid open and sniffed the liquid.

"Yeah, that's some ancient diesel." Reins closed the lid and searched the pile of junk for a funnel. He was in luck – lying at the bottom was just what he needed. "I'm going to look for the generators." Around the corner he discovered a small corral where a multitude of electrical cables connected it to the main building of the station. He picked the lock and went in.

The two generators that had once powered the station had run dry to the point where it would be difficult to restart them in this cold weather. Nevertheless, Reins filled one of the generators up and checked if the starter battery still had power. He pressed the *ON* switch and soon the sound of an old engine cranking filled the shed.

"Generator's back online." Reins pumped his fist. "Though I only have a gallon of fuel running it."

"There should be a fuse box connected to the generators. Open it and switch off any non-essential systems to save fuel. We'll need all the time we can get to download those files."

Reins made his way back inside and found the main office where the higher-ranked officials would have worked and plugged his PDA into the electronic lock.

"I'm hooked in," Reins said. Someone back at base hacked the device. Moments later it was unlocked and he made his way inside. He found the main computer and booted it up. Before long, it too was hacked into and the files were set to download.

"We've got the files," Hanson said. "I'll prowl through them and get back to you with an update, ASAP. Get some R&R."

Reins cleared one corner of the room and created a barricade with a few tables and chairs before emptying his backpack. He opened one of his ration packs and began warming his food on the small portable stove. After filling his stomach, he rested in the corner of the room and checked the status of his suit. Seventy-two percent battery remained. He switched the heated pads off to conserve power and nodded off with his rifle in hand.

* * *

"Reins?" Hanson called out, waking the ranger from his slumber.

"Yeah?" Reins yawned and shivered. The cold had pierced his suit. Glancing at the time on his visor, he calculated he'd been asleep for a few hours. According to his PDA it was night.

"Good, you're awake. We've gone through the files and have an interesting update for you."

"What did you find?" Reins asked, switching his suit's heating back on whilst setting up the stove to make himself a nice warm cup of tea.

"Looks like they were conducting an excavation in the nearby cave system. Whilst digging they found what they describe as 'an ancient artefact'. After running it through a series of tests, they determined that it was made from an unknown element. Estimates for its age had come back at being over three million years old with the report concluding it was not of this world."

"Right, well, we know that there are other worlds out there," Reins said. Hell, he'd been to some of them on past missions.

"That we do, but nothing like this. Anyway, they brought the artefact back to base and began doing further experiments on it. It was then some of the staff started showing strange behaviour. Severe headaches and nausea ran rampant throughout the base before reports of shadowy figures and mysterious voices. Then a final security report states that they'd set fire to the vehicles and destroyed the fuel supplies before going to check on a strange noise in the adjacent room."

"We've fought demons before but this doesn't sound like one. I think we might be dealing with something new here," Reins said, adding 'not sure if that's better or worse' to himself as he gulped down his warm tea. "Let me check the other room and see what they found."

"All right, make your way there and radio back once you have discovered more."

Reins removed the barricade he had erected and made his way to the next room. When his comrade had hacked the main office door, he'd also unlocked all the other doors in the station. Which was just as well, since the power had died out whilst he slept. The door swung open and he walked in.

The walls were covered in dried crusty blood, and about the floor were strewn intestines and other internal organs. But strangely, there were no bodies. *What the fuck am I dealing with?* Reins thought to himself.

"Hanson, are you seeing this?"

"I see it. Just confirms that the artefact we're dealing with is extremely dangerous. I suggest you proceed with caution. You might find more answers in the cave system where they found it. I'm sending the co-ordinates over now."

"Shouldn't I wait till morning before setting off?"

"Negative. I've just been advised there's a storm on the way. You have about nine hours before it hits the station."

"Damn! Going to be a tough journey but I should have enough power in the suit to make it work."

After a short yet arduous journey, Reins approached the mouth of the rocky opening at the foot of a small mountain, and cautiously walked down the steep ramp into its dark depths, rifle at the ready. He made sure the main lights on his suit were off and switched to night vision on his visor. It would drain even more power but he needed it for a stealthy situation such as this.

In the shelter of the ancient cave system at the foot of the ramp, countless footprints filled the uneven floor, leading him further into the unknown. He entered a larger cavern where he immediately noticed a flat-topped rocky platform. A strangely luminescent shard of some green rock or metal sat upon it. He guessed that was the artefact. The floor was littered with the frozen, naked bodies of the research crew. They had been torn limb from limb. Bite marks and other horrific wounds covered what remained.

Reins walked among the mess of bodies, casting his infra-red light from side to side. He paused. Frowning, he crouched and traced his gloved finger along a series of thin grooves in the rocky floor. It looked like something large had been dragged further into the cave. Standing again, he tracked the grooves with his light. His eyes bulged and he took a step back when he saw the thing at the rear of the chamber, wreathed in an emerald smog.

"Jesus!" he hissed, his voice echoing in the darkness around him.

It was massive, and repulsive. A huge dark bloated body was supported by four powerful squat limbs that ended in vicious clawed feet. A multitude of tentacles writhed and slapped wetly against its slick leathery body as it turned its oblong-shaped head in Reins' direction. Eyes – too many eyes – glowed and blinked in the green light.

Without warning, the artefact pulsed and some of the emerald smog coalesced between a pair of larger tentacles, and the creature hurled the globule of thick supernatural energy towards him. Reins ducked and rolled away, narrowly avoiding the spray of rocky shards. He had encountered magic before and even knew how to use certain spells himself but this beast gave off a particular sour aura that was new to him. However, he guessed the artefact was its power source.

Fighting this thing in the cave would be futile; his night

vision was limited and left him vulnerable. He turned and ran toward the pedestal between him and the entrance as the creature shot more energy towards the dead bodies surrounding the artefact, almost crashing into him again. He saw thin tendrils of green energy flow from the artefact towards the bodies and, as he watched in horror, the limbs began to randomly join together and reanimate in jerky spasms.

"Fuck!" Reins cursed. He had to retrieve the artefact *right now* and get the hell out of the cave.

He raised his weapon and fired into the crowd of grotesque constructs with standard issue silver-imbued bullets, clearing a temporary path to the artefact. But even as he drew nearer to his goal, the bullet-ridden monstrosities began to twitch and rise again. He kicked out and clubbed a few aside with his rifle, and then he was momentarily free of assailants.

Reins reached out and grabbed the shard but almost dropped it when his arm was engulfed in the green smog. His combat suit did its job; the defensive wards prepared back at base now effectively countered the attack. He stuffed the shard into a pocket. He had a suitable containment bag in his backpack and would put it in there once he got back to the base – *if* he got back to the base. An ominous scraping and gurgling sounded from behind him.

Emptying his magazine, he cleared another path to the exit and sprinted away from the pedestal, risking a glance over his shoulder. The creature was close – looming over him, upper tentacles brushing against the roof of the cavern, dislodging stalactites as it lumbered after him.

He didn't think silver bullets would help him against that big bastard, but the falling stalactites had given him an idea – a risky and dangerous one. He'd use his own magic to slow it down, regardless of the personal cost.

Clubbing aside another of the shambling constructs that

intercepted him at the bottom of the ramp, Reins stooped, tugged off a glove and placed a fingertip on the icy floor. With a calm urgency, he carefully inscribed a pattern on the rock, a red aura trailing from his finger. With one final motion, the trap was laid. He hurried up the ramp, waded out into the snow, panting hard, and turned to see the results.

"Hanson, come in!" he shouted into his comms.

"What is it?"

"We may have a small issue. The artefact has reanimated the research staff and summoned some kind of massive creature. Silver is not doing a damn thing. I've laid a fire trap, though I don't know how effective it's going to be." He could see the lesser abominations shuffling up the ramp, a large shadow behind them close to his handiwork. "It should be powerful enough to destroy the entrance of the cave but I don't know if it's going to hold that big fucker back."

"Damn it. I was hoping this mission was going to go smoothly. Secure the artefact and make your way back to the research station. Back-up's on its way." The connection clicked off.

The trap triggered a huge explosion, the shockwave nearly knocking the ranger off his feet. The cave mouth crumbled, burying the bodies of the reanimated corpses. Reins opened his backpack and secured the artefact in the containment bag before heading for the base. As he did, deep growls erupted from the buried entrance and more rocks began to crack and crumble; the creature was attempting to escape. His earlier worries were correct, the stone barricade wouldn't hold it back for long. Damn, sometimes he hated being proved right. He picked up the pace, weary limbs complaining.

Reins approached the main doors of the base and checked the status of his suit. It was just under fifty percent – enough to last him until the next day. He entered the building, dropping his backpack on the floor of the main office with a sigh.

"How long until back-up arrives?" Reins asked between heavy breaths. He needed to get some energy back into his body to replenish what he'd used to power the magic, so he quickly warmed some food on the stove while he waited for a response from Colonel Hanson to break through the static noise on his radio. The wind could be heard picking up outside, a sure sign that a blizzard was brewing.

"You'll have to hold out until the weather calms," Hanson finally replied. "It's going to be hard getting more boots on the ground."

Reins sat down in a corner of the room and slowly ate through his MRE pack. His mind was fatigued as well as his bones and muscles. Foggy visions of the creature swam through his tired mind, filling him with deep dread and a sense of imminent doom. He was knackered but sleep wasn't an option with that colossal thing still walking around out there...

A loud thud awoke him from his slumber. The blur of momentary confusion was quickly replaced with sharply focused memories of the thing in the cave. He heard more noises that sounded like furniture being scraped across a hard floor. Someone was moving around in the canteen. Was it the back-up team? A deep, too familiar throaty growl put paid to that thought.

"Shit!" Reins said, pushing himself to his feet. He switched his suit into stealth mode, replacing the magazine in his rifle with incendiary rounds. "Time to party," he whispered, before rushing out into the corridor.

The growls got louder as he crept closer to the canteen doorway, keeping his back against the wall. He paused and took a few deep breaths as he steeled himself. It sounded like it was rearranging the room in there. Shit, the thing was powerful.

How the hell had it got in? The sound of the storm had grown louder as he'd approached – that was a big clue. "This is it, Reins. Time for the last stand," he whispered, and stepped out into the doorway.

It seemed even bigger in the confines of the ruins of the room before him. The upper torso and two legs were inside the canteen where they'd smashed in through the roof; the rest of it was still outside, framed against the billowing snowstorm. The monster's oblong head swung around and the rows of vivid green eyes stared at him. There was a malicious intelligence in them that he'd not noticed in the dark cave. Something else he'd not noticed before was a widening maw, filled with rows of glistening fangs.

Reins shook away his feeling of impotence and raised his weapon, letting loose a long volley of rounds at the creature's head. Every bullet hit the target in tight grouping. The creature reared up, wailing in agony as the bullets burned through its unnatural leathery skin, leaving fire-rimmed holes that wept a dark grey substance which Reins presumed was its blood.

"Looks like you have a weakness to fire." Reins smiled grimly, stepping back and reloading. The creature's green eyes fixed on him once more, glowing with hatred.

It lashed out, swinging its tentacles towards him, long sharp talons protruding out of the slimy skin. Reins barely rolled out of the way in time, though he doubted his armour would stand a chance as the doorframe and walls cracked and splintered under the thrashing tentacles.

"You're going to have to do better than that, you slimy bastard," Reins yelled before taking a kneeling stance and unloading another magazine into the creature. The thing's scream of pain gargled into a bellow of rage. He knew he'd need to up his game to defeat it. There were two heavy duty incendiary grenades in his backpack but he had left it back in the office. He traced another firetrap rune on the corridor floor just outside the doorway and then sprinted away. Reins knew he'd feel the full cost soon, but it would be worth it to slow the thing down.

He was almost at the office door when the wall to his left exploded in shards of flying plaster, wood and steel. He curled into a tight ball as a wall of flame washed over him, then scrambled to his feet seconds later as the heat subsided.

A tentacle crashed through the ceiling and flopped over his shoulder. He yelped in surprise and leaped back, swatting at the dark grey limb with the barrel of his rifle. The tentacle fell to the floor and lay twitching, the ragged end splashing more blood onto the dusty floor. With a deafening roar, the rest of the creature smashed its way into the corridor; badly lacerated head swinging from side to side, searching for its tormentor.

"You've got to be fucking kidding me..." Reins said. He turned and ran to the office.

Slinging his rifle over his shoulder after reloading again, he fished out the grenades and rushed back out into the half-demolished corridor, leaving his backpack behind. It would only slow him down.

He realised the trap had done significant damage to the creature as it limped towards him. In addition to numerous missing tentacles, one of its legs was badly messed up and dragged uselessly as it squeezed itself down the passage towards him. It may have been in great pain but it was still alive and angrier than ever before. He would need to act fast if he was going to kill the fucking thing. First of all, he'd need more space to work in.

Reins leaped out of the large outer door and into the raging snowstorm outside. He stumbled away from the entrance. The creature was close behind him; he could hear it growling. He turned to see how close and stood in awe as it began to drag its huge bulk through the metal doorframe.

He pulled the pin on one of the grenades, hurling it in a high arc towards the creature, and back-peddled as it detonated in a fierce ball of flames. The creature screamed and fell forward into the snow, flesh burning and dribbling from its bones. It lay still, skin crackling and blistering in the super-heated inferno for a few moments before the smoke and sound was whipped away into the strong gusts of freezing wind. Reins' legs gave way and he slipped to the ground.

"Hanson?" Reins gasped into his comms, sitting in the snow and panting hard. He was knackered, totally drained – the cost of the magic finally catching up with him. But the creature was dead and all he wanted to do now was report back and then go to sleep.

"I know," Hanson replied. "I've been watching your feed. Great job fighting the creature. I have a bird in the air, so start prepping for evac."

Reins was about to answer when a searing pain lanced through his lower leg. He yelped and tried to pull away, staring down at the tentacle that gripped his ankle and the razor-sharp point that sliced open his suit and skin. Eyes following the appendage back to its source, he struggled harder to break free. The creature crawled towards him, its skeleton and inner organs poking out through its half-melted body. It moved closer, dragging Reins slowly towards its wide, slobbering mouth.

The second thermal grenade had slipped from his grasp as he'd tried to tear off the tightening tendril. Now he glanced around, desperately trying to locate it as the creature hauled him a few feet towards its blood and saliva streaked jaws. The grenade lay in the snow behind him – in a second it would be out of reach. Summoning all of his remaining strength, Reins flung himself full-length, twisting as he did so. His grasping hand closed around the grenade and he slipped a thumb into the pin.

Spinning back around, he realised the thing had relaxed its hold on his leg as it sought to gain a better grip. Kicking free, he sat up and rammed his fist into the thing's mouth, the reinforced glove splintering a couple of teeth in the process. "Chew on that!" Reins hissed, releasing his final grenade. He rolled over and scrambled away while he could.

The explosion shook the earth. Reins was thrown like a rag doll, spiralling through the air and coming to rest against the wall of an outbuilding. His visor was cracked and the combat suit compromised in a number of places, but he was alive. That was more than could be said for the monstrous horror. It was merely a mound of shattered bones and shredded flesh. Its head was gone – remnants of it strewn all around him in glistening splashes of gore.

Reins looked down at his leg. It was still bleeding, turning the pure white snow a deep crimson. But the cold had numbed most of the pain and he was too tired to go back for his med-pack. He sighed and rested his head against the wall. Within a few moments he could hear the welcoming hum of the helicopter once again. The pilot put it down not too far from the headless creature. A couple of guys helped him aboard, and soon a medic was tending to his wounds.

Now that the area was secure, a couple of guys from the recovery team went to retrieve the artefact and search through the office for any details he'd missed. While Reins watched, the others wrapped the remains of the creature up and tied it to the landing skids of the helicopter; it would be taken back to the labs for a thorough autopsy.

Feeling a little better now, Reins dug a cigarette out of a ripped pocket and lit up, taking in a deep breath.

"Oi, no smoking!" the pilot shouted.

"Fuck off," Reins replied, taking a deep drag of the smoke and savouring the warming calm that swept over him. A few seconds later, the cigarette was torn from his fingers, the glowing tip quickly extinguished. He closed his eyes and took a moment to simply feel the bitter cold of the Antarctic raging around him. It was far from comfortable, but he wasn't complaining about that now. He'd done it. Reins was alive, and the enemy was defeated. The mission had been another success, and he would return home triumphant once again.

AQIB ALI

Aqib Ali is an author from Huddersfield, West Yorkshire. He enjoys writing short stories, novellas, novels and creating audio-books. He is currently working on the third episode of his Supernatural Dark Fantasy series The Dark Ranger. He also regularly posts creative writing  and helpful content on both his blog and facebook page.

Check his website/blog
http://www.aqibaliauthor.com/
Or follow his Social Media channels below

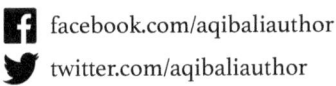 facebook.com/aqibaliauthor
twitter.com/aqibaliauthor

THE PIT

"SOMETIMES IT'S JUST ABOUT GETTING
THROUGH THE DAY."

CM ANGUS

"Can I have a biscuit?"

The question, so normal yet so alien, surprises me, catches me off-guard, and fills me with doubt.

I know it is directed at me, but how am I supposed to answer?

The crushing weight returns to my chest and I only just manage to croak a response.

"What?"

The small boy again points to the chipped ceramic pot on the kitchen worktop.

"A biscuit. Please can I have one, Dad?"

Pressure flows into my face, unseen fingers digging their way into my sinuses. My eyes screw up as I attempt to concentrate.

> *For fuck's sake!*
> *It's not like it's the biggest decision in the world.*
> *Why can't I respond?*
> *Why am I so fucking broken?*
> *What-the-shitting-fuck-is-wrong-with-me?*

Tear ducts well as I grunt a reply.

"Can you ask your mother?"

I crawl away to hide – refuse to be an adult.

> *Is this useless fucking cunt really me?*

But it is me, and while it is not *always* me, it's me often enough.

And when it is, I wear the face of another man to tell the world that everything is all right, that everything is fine.

I say that I'm taking it easy and that I have everything I need.

Rather that than face a breakdown simply because the shop is out of Cherry fucking Coke.

I exist only to *just about* cope in this moment. For now, I have no past, I have no future and am unable to be the grown up.

I turn on the bath taps and while the tub fills, I take a shit, hoping not to somehow fuck that up as well.

> *What if I don't fix this?*
> *What about the house?*
> *What about the mortgage!*

I'm immersed in the bath now but it is no better. The feelings just won't stop. The incessant chatter of thought after thought continues unabated. All of them urgent, all of them gibberish. I wince as my anxiety grows.

I don't know if it's the heat of the water or the pounding of my chest but I feel nauseous, I feel faint and my hands begin to throb.

> *Why does nothing I do work?*
> *Fuck this!*

I'm in bed when the tears come, and once they come, they don't stop. They come, and they come, and they come. I hear myself scream inside my head and watch myself rip at my hair.

> *Who is this?*
> *I don't even recognize who I am anymore.*
> *Where am I?*
> *Who am I?*
> *Where-the-fuck will all this end?*
> *I am angst.*

I am mine own private dread.
Alone and adrift on an endless ocean of despair.

The sound of the door opening.
"Can I have another biscuit – please?"

I am the pit.

CM ANGUS

Born and raised in a steel-town in the Northeast of England, CM Angus now lives in Yorkshire with his better half, his children and an awesome dog.

With a background in e-Commerce and technology, his work is inquisitive and blends a passion for story telling with a strong scientific grounding. He is currently working on Fixpoint, a series of books with each piece tackling different aspects of discontinuities in time and is a Speculative Fiction spanning 4 generations of a family haunted by the prospect of an approaching alternate reality where their child has been erased from history.

Overstrike, Volume 1 of Fixpoint, was published by Elsewhen Press in 2020.

Follow CM Angus at https://cmangus.blogspot.com or via his Social Media Channels.

amazon.com/author/cmangus
facebook.com/author.cm.angus
twitter.com/c_m_angus
instagram.com/author.cm.angus
goodreads.com/cm_angus

SHADOW COMPANY

"A SCIFI SPEC-OPS TEAM FIND MORE THAN
THEY EXPECTED WHEN RETRIEVING A
PACKAGE ON A WAR-TORN WORLD."

GARETH CLEGG

Landing in a hot DZ is never much fun, but today was a bad one, and I've done a lot of combat drops. Tactical launches from orbit were the worst, packed into a missile casing and fired at the drop zone like a bullet. Fifteen seconds of high Gs bouncing inside a tin can, designed to break on impact, isn't my first choice for entering a mission. But we'd trained for this and were all G-monsters, capable of withstanding the violent descent and arriving ready for immediate action. Ash loved it; the thrill of the ride he called it. But he was the guy who enjoyed throwing a parachute off something tall and leaping after it, hoping he'd get it on and open before the ground leapt up to welcome him. Call me old-fashioned, but I'd rather airlift in and hike twenty klicks to the target. Maybe I was getting too old for all this shit.

The cocoon blew apart on impact, thrusting me out into the blasted landscape of what was once a city. Smoke drifted through the rubble-strewn streets from collapsed buildings everywhere. Nothing left stood much above ten storeys. The blue shock-gel sloughed from my body, losing its integrity as I hit the ground. They said it protected us from being crushed into pieces, but my knees always felt like hell for the first few minutes after deployment. I suppose it was a small price to pay for insertion from orbit in seconds.

A large section of shattered plascrete lay close to my left, and I slid into its protective embrace before hailing the team. "Squad sound off."

"Pitbull, checking weapon systems. Good to go."

"Ash here. Things are peachy, just eighty-sixed a few nosy drones."

"Reaper, scanning for tangos. Looks clear."

I waited a moment for the final report. "Angel? What's your twenty?"

"Still climbing, Sarge. In position in fifteen seconds."

"Okay, ping me a tactical when you're topside."

"Roger that."

Good as her word, the data pinged through, details of the ruined city growing on the tac-map as she swept the area with her scoped rifle.

"Ash," I called into the inbuilt comms. "Tell me more about those drones."

His dulcet tones filled my head. "Everything's cool. They're standard recon models, just a little too close for comfort. It'll look like they caught some stray fire and went down."

"Roger that. Keep me updated when we move on our target."

"Will do."

The map was taking shape, with our objective illuminated in red as I spun the 3D construct in my HUD. The building seemed in reasonable condition compared to the taller ruins surrounding it – looked like they'd taken most of the flak during the siege. "How are things topside, Angel?"

"Yeah, looks good so far. They've focused their forces on the perimeter against the main assault; not much internal security in the streets, but there's a lot of intervening buildings. I can't cover you to the doors from here."

"Understood. Follow us in, best speed." I fed in a route which popped onto the map, a series of marching blue ants showing our planned course. "You happy with that?"

"Sure," Angel replied. "Give me five to reposition, then you're good to go."

"Roger that." A timer began ticking in the corner of my view. "Okay, squad. This is gonna be slow and steady, picking our way through at street level. Pitbull, we've got too many hazards between us and the target to utilise your artillery. Switch to the heavy fifties."

He snorted. "Agreed." As much as he adored his man-portable missile system, he knew this wasn't the arena for them. And even though he bitched about them, he loved rolling out the mini-guns. At two thousand rounds per minute, they were real street sweepers.

I waited for the blip from Angel, showing she was in position before proceeding. "Okay, standard formation. Check those buildings for hostiles and let's move out."

We'd done this a hundred times before, perhaps more. Each of the squad were seasoned operators from tier-one outfits, and I trusted each of them with my life. We picked our way through the rubble-choked streets, checking all the angles before progressing further. I took point. Yeah, I know it's not the done thing – leading from the front – but this was my speciality, and the others knew it.

Before taking command, they'd all called me 'Nose'. I'd had a sixth sense for sniffing out danger, but now I was just 'Sarge'. I missed the old days of not having to keep this rabble in order, but someone had to step into the role, and I seemed best suited to wear the dead man's shoes.

I knelt at the corner of an intersection, hugging the cracked remains of a building, and waved the others over. Ash and Reaper crossed the distance at a walk, almost nonchalant to the uninformed observer, but they were both tech-heavy, systems scanning the area for anything untoward. Once they took position behind me, we waited for Pitbull to lumber over, servo's hissing as they propelled the man-mountain to us. He didn't need to check his six; the others were on that, while I checked our route onward.

"Take the next left, Sarge," Angel said. "There's a lot of rubble straight ahead that you'll have to crawl over."

"Roger that, Angel," I said, adjusting our course. The blue ants twitched as I pushed the change out to the squad.

Hell, but it felt good having a pair of eyes in the skies, especially when you added Angel's supporting firepower into the equation. Let's just say her ability to take down almost any enemy at two klicks was one reason we'd survived as long as we had. Yeah, we'd lost members over time, but that's how it goes in this life. When it hits the fan, it helps if you're fucking good at your job, but sometimes it's just down to dumb luck.

A massive crack echoed above us before Angel called, "Debris – take cover."

We all huddled close to the building wall as Angel's video feed showed rubble pouring from a pall of smoke some eight storeys above. The ground shook as a ten-metre slab slammed into it, spitting rocks and pebbles which spanged from our armoured bodies. A few smaller sections rained down onto the road, and then it was just dust and scree.

"You guys okay down there?"

"Good to go," I replied, the other three giving me thumbs-ups after checking their gear. "Let's move out before any more of this comes down. Did you get eyes on the impact, Angel?"

"Yeah, looked like a stray inbound missile on the replay."

"What the fuck are they firing into the centre for?" Reaper said. "Don't they know they've got boots down here?"

Ash laughed. "Yeah, we're real precious. The brass always gives special orders not to fire near operators on the ground doing the dirty work."

All it took was two words from me. "Okay, enough." The casual command brought everyone back to business in an instant as we followed the alternative route to our objective.

As we approached the final corner, Angel's voice echoed over the comms. "Sarge, what exactly are we supposed to be retrieving?"

"No specifics," I replied. "Just a package. Why, what are you seeing?"

A video window opened in my HUD. A squat building that looked like a fortified bunker popped into focus. Emblazoned across the entrance were the words 'Medical Research Centre'.

* * *

The approach to the grey-walled building was clear of enemy units, and we crossed towards the glass-fronted entrance. The damned place looked like a hospital, though a little dirty from the dust that hung in the air throughout the city.

"No security?" Ash asked. "What the hell are these jokers playing at?"

I picked my way through the mass of abandoned vehicles. A thick layer of grime coated them, but glimpses of bright reds and blues shone beneath their grey shrouds.

Four bodies lay slumped on the white-tiled floor beyond the main doors. "Reaper, check this out."

He peered through the plexiglass, tapping into his arm-mounted scanner. "Robotic combat units; no obvious signs of damage, except a bit of scorching. I'd say something fried their circuits."

I motioned to the nearest one, just the other side of the glass. "We haven't thrown any EMP this way, have we?"

Reaper shrugged. "Not that I'm aware of. Surely the brass would have told you?"

I shook my head. "Nothing in the mission intel."

The dark interior reinforced the power overload scenario and, as I touched the door, it didn't budge.

The others took up defensive positions as I jammed my fingers between the sliding doors, forcing them open a crack, but it was hard going. "Pitbull, a little help?"

Seven feet of heavy plated armour stomped forward as I unslung my rifle to cover him. "I could just blow the glass," he said, and the mini-guns began that low whine as the barrels spun up to speed.

"Whoa there, big guy. Let's keep this quiet." I tapped him on the shoulder. "For now."

He was always eager to play with his toys, but he was a model soldier: solid, dependable and taking orders without complaint. The rotation slowed, noise fading as he stepped close to the entrance. His thick armoured fingers forced into the gap, pushing the protesting doors aside with ease. "There ya go, Sarge."

The chemical cleansers hit us as we entered – that smell you find in all hospitals. The foyer looked much like any other medical establishment, though it seemed in reasonable condition compared to the other buildings in this part of town. Other than the four RCU's at the entrance, there were no signs of life. While our tech checked the bodies, I located the only other exit; a pair of lifts on the far side of the room. My shoulder-mounted lamp threw bright arcs of light around the place as I headed back to see if there was more to learn from the remains. "Pitbull, Ash, check if you can get those lift doors open."

They nodded, beams flashing across the area as they moved. "Anything new?" I called to Reaper.

He shook his head. "No, just confirmation of a huge electronic overload. Everything, and I mean everything, got fried. Look."

Melted plastic and blobs of molten metal were all that remained of the electrical connections and circuit boards. I was no expert, but I'd never come across anything like this before. "What could cause this?"

"Short of a massive EMP discharge, and I'm talking capital ship tech, I can't tell you. I'll check the facility power grid, but I'm expecting more of the same."

"Salvage?"

He laughed. "The physical stuff – armour, actuators, muscle fibre – it's all pristine. But not a chance with anything electrical."

"Okay, review the grid, then meet us at the lift."

I stalked across the room, leaving our tech scratching his head. "Give me some good news, Ash."

"No can do, Sarge. There's nothing to work with. The power is out on everything, so no systems to hack or bypass."

"Damn it. Can you brute force it?"

A deep bass rumble came from Pitbull – laughter. "Sure thing, boss. But it ain't gonna be quiet."

Ash glanced up. "Me and Pit thought you'd prefer to know before we blew anything up."

"Good call, but let's get it open. The package is on sub-level two. Angel?"

"Here, Sarge."

"Find yourself somewhere comfortable with a view. I need to hear as soon as there is any change topside. We don't want to come out with the package to a company of bad-tempered hombre's waiting to take it from us."

"Understood."

Angel wasn't one for small talk. Straight to the point, then onto her next objective. She didn't say much about herself, and I knew nothing of her off-duty activities, what she did with her downtime, or if she even had friends outside the squad.

A squeal of grinding metal turned me back to the lift where Pitbull wrenched the thick lift doors apart, revealing a dark chasm descending into the heart of the complex.

"Angel's staying topside," I said, moving to inspect the drop.

Reaper pointed into the shaft. "Rappelling gear is in situ; it will be quicker than climbing ladders. Sub-level two is down there, about thirty metres. We should be able to gain access from there."

"Good work. I'll head down with Pitbull; we'll call you once we've secured the doorway."

"I hate rappelling," Pitbull said, turning to Reaper. "You sure this is strong enough for me?"

The tech laughed. "Yeah, that heavy cable of yours could support a battle tank."

"That's great, but I was talking about the anchor point."

"Well, now you mention it," Reaper said, rubbing his chin, "it looks a bit rusty. Might be too much for a BFU."

Pitbull's head leant to one side. "BFU?"

"Big Fucking Unit," Reaper replied with a laugh. "Hell, man, it's safe. It will hold you without a problem. Now clip on and get down the fucking hole like a good dog."

Pitbull was difficult to gauge. He sometimes came across as slow, but I got the feeling it was just an act. There was no doubting his loyalty. He'd thrust himself into the line of fire to protect other members of the squad many times, and even though they teased him, it was all in good humour.

I clipped my cord into the carabiner with a reassuring clunk. "Okay, enough. Time to get to work." I stepped into the void, and the darkness consumed me as the cable whirred out above.

* * *

The doors to sub-level two parted with much less effort than the ones above. I pulled myself out of the shaft while Pitbull hung there, rotary cannons ready to lay waste to anything he didn't like the look of.

A long corridor stretched out in my torchlight, stopping as it passed over more collapsed bodies before a security door. "More tangos down here. They seem inert." I scanned with my rifle, tracking the rest of the hallway.

"On my way," Reaper said, the humming of his fast descent slowing as he appeared beside Pitbull and swung over to the hall. He started toward the nearest doorway while I knelt, covering his advance.

"Power's out," he whispered, his message enhanced by the comm system as he tried the door. "Locked."

By the time he got to the next one, Ash stood by me in the corridor. I walked forward to help check the remaining doors. They were all sealed, and we moved to the bodies where Reaper's scans showed them flatlined like the bots above.

As I reached to examine the security door, Reaper's hand fell on my shoulder. "Whoa, there's still power to that."

"Ash, you're up," I called, as we pulled back to cover him while he worked his magic.

"Wow, that's heavy tech, Sarge," he said. "Way beyond standard military encryption."

"Can you crack it?"

"Hell, yes. Might take a few minutes."

I nodded and let him go to work. This was where Ash excelled. Anything to do with computers and security and he was in his element. He could even do a half-decent job working with mechanical components and often helped Reaper with salvage.

The door opened an inch, sliding and grinding for a moment, before recessing into the wall. Red emergency lights lined the ceiling every twenty feet as the corridor fled into the darkness. A security station held another two fried bots and a host of monitors, all blank. I nodded for Ash to investigate while I stalked forward, motioning Reaper to follow.

Sturdy looking doors stood on opposite sides of the walls, each with a small red light, pulsing with a soft glow.

"Ash, what have you got?" I called.

"Power is real low. I'm bypassing systems to get more juice, but it looks like a detention centre."

"Any idea where our package might be?"

"Well, if I had to guess, I'd aim for cell twelve. It has the strongest encryption and multiple active feeds."

I nodded to Reaper, and we edged forward till we reached number twelve. Where the other cells had dull flashing red lights, this one was solid and bright. We prepped for standard doorway entry, and I gave Ash the go signal. Our preparations were over the top for what we saw when the door recessed into the ground. The cell was only just long enough to fit a narrow bed, where a young girl, wrapped in a rough blanket, hugged her knees. The smell in there was appalling, and as I panned the light around the cramped space, it highlighted an overflowing wall-mounted toilet.

Reaper turned his head to me, keeping his weapon trained on the figure. "This is the package? What the hell do we want with a child?"

"Ash, is this the only secure cell down here?" I asked.

"It's the only one with active power from the back-up grid."

I returned my gaze to the girl, and she thrust her hand out, shielding her eyes. I reduced the intensity of the light, aiming it down at her feet. "Hey, it's okay. We're here to get you out. Can you walk?"

After a moment, she nodded, the short blonde bob waving before settling in a diagonal stripe across her face, hiding her left eye. I guessed early teens by the size of her, though the oversized white jumpsuit made her look more like a scientist in an ill-fitting lab coat.

Her legs wobbled as she pushed herself from the bed, and she had to grab the wall, but after a few moments, she took a hesitant step toward me. I stretched out my hand. "What's your name?"

Her face creased in concentration, then she shrugged, pointing to the number twelve on her suit.

"No real name, huh? You're gonna fit in just fine with us misfits. I'm Sarge and this," I motioned to my side, "is Reaper. He needs to run a few medical checks on you."

The girl pulled away, slipping on the slick floor, scrambling for the safety of her blanket on the bed.

"Whoa, it's okay. He won't hurt you, he's like a doctor. I just want him to check that you are fit enough to walk out of here with us."

She cowered in the corner, emitting a high-pitched keening, while rocking back and forth clutching her knees, knuckles white.

"It's fine, Sarge. I've got plenty from the scans. She's dehydrated and borderline malnourished, but other than that she looks in reasonable shape. Nothing a few square meals wouldn't fix."

"Hey, Twelve? You don't need any tests. Everything's okay; we can leave now. We'll take you somewhere safe, how does that sound?"

I had no experience talking with kids. What the hell was I supposed to do with a terrified girl who'd been through God knows what in this medical research centre? I wasn't squeamish, but the thought of some crazy scientists poking around at this kid – enough to terrify her at the mention of a doctor – worried me. What the fuck had they been up to? And why all the secrecy about the identity of the package? I didn't enjoy guessing games, and this was feeling fucked up.

The comms crackled with a signal trying to get through. I boosted the gain and cleaned it up enough to catch Angel's voice the second time around.

"Sarge, do you read?"

"Go ahead, Angel. Had a bit of interference, but I'm reading you now."

"You need to haul ass. We've got multiple ground troops converging on your position, ETA five minutes. I'll do what I can to slow them down, but there's a lot of them."

"Roger that. Squad, move out."

I turned to the girl, holding out my hand again. "If you want to leave, we have to go now. The people who run this place are coming back."

That was enough. She grabbed hold and almost dragged me toward the lift, pointing upward with her free hand.

"Yep," I said. "We're getting out of here, double time."

* * *

The rest of the team were already topside when I reached the foyer. Say what you like about ascent systems, they sure as hell beat trying to climb thirty metres in full combat load-out with a scared kid dangling from your neck.

I'd heard half a dozen shots from outside as Angel laid down some death from above.

The tac-map pinged as new red targets popped into view from the north-east. Angel was one step ahead of me as an escape route danced on-screen, heading south, then west. As well as slowing the approaching forces, she was pathfinding for us too. Damn, but she was gunning for MVP again.

Dust drifted to the ground as near-misses rocked the building.

"Sarge, you need to hightail it now; they've mobilised artillery." Angel's calm voice held the slightest hint of tension, but that's about as ruffled as she ever got.

"Roger that, Angel. We felt the tremors, but we're clear." Three fresh targets lit on the tac-map as I pushed through the doorway and between the parked cars. "Pitbull, time to get busy. Let's lose those big guns."

"Yes, sir," Pitbull growled. His missile pods activated, arching up from his back and spreading like wings above his shoulders. The ground leapt beneath us as the micro-missiles screamed into the air, spiralling toward their targets.

We ran, following the trail marked on our HUDs. The grainy video feed whited out as the enemy launchers exploded. The deep bass thump, from over a klick away, shook the street.

"That's one mighty fine crater you made," Angel said. "But we've got troops moving through the streets."

"I'm on it," Pitbull replied. His heavy footfalls halted behind us as he reloaded with P9os, the readout on my HUD showing his fire plan as he homed in on Angel's markers.

The 'Proxies' were a nasty piece of hardware, delivering hundreds of micro proximity mines over a wide area. They were made for situations like this, where we were trying to bug out of a hot zone.

The kid shifted, squirming about and mumbling something incoherent. My rifle's maglocks clicked as I attached it to my side, and I took a better grip on Twelve, squeezing her tight to my chest. As long as any incoming was from behind, my armour would protect her.

"Where's the extraction, Angel?" I asked, seeing no marker on the tac-map.

"We've got a heavy bird inbound; just getting coordinates now." A blue cross flashed beyond the city limits.

"Fuck, that's two klicks outside the walls," Reaper said. "They think we need the exercise or what?"

"Embrace the suck, squad," I replied. "Bitching about the XP won't bring it any closer."

Angel appeared up ahead as she leapt from one rooftop to another, heading for ground level as we approached the outskirts. She moved like an athlete, light recon armour causing no hindrance as she shifted between cover.

"How's the wall looking, Angel?" I called, hoping for some good news.

"Solid at the moment, but that shouldn't be a problem for long. HV incoming; prepare for breach."

Dust and debris leapt from the ground as an ominous shadow passed overhead, its four huge rotors almost deafening as the heavy transport thundered by. We took cover as two missiles dropped from either side of the beast, their rockets flaring to life and streaking to the wall ahead. The explosion bathed us with scorching air for an instant, and we pushed through the concussion wave into the swirling smoke.

"Is that our ride, Angel?" I called as the HVI banked, curving toward the west.

"Yeah, she's setting down at the XP."

"I still don't see why we have to run so far. She could have set down right there," Reaper said, pointing just outside the shattered wall.

"When was your last medical?" I asked. "Maybe command thinks you need to focus more on your cardio?"

This brought a chuckle from the rest of the squad as we pushed on. The missiles had made quick work of the city's protective boundary, shredding it like paper. Sections of smouldering plascrete lay scattered beyond a ragged hole in the wall. We slowed to pick our way through the rubble, then regained speed, heading west towards rockier ground.

For all his bellyaching, I had to admit Reaper had a point. Why had they sent an assault ship to extract us? It packed enough punch to ignore any weaponry the enemy could bring to bear on it, other than more of that artillery. Though they called it a transport, this was a beast of war, designed to deploy heavy units to the front and to show enemies just who they were fucking with. The thing bristled with large calibre railguns and missile pods. It was a mobile fortress.

All we needed was a fast ship with space for us and the package, though she took almost no room at all. Something was wrong. I smelled trouble, and the itch inside my head told me it would be a problem.

"Ash, go secure," I said, waiting for his confirmation.

A few seconds later, I received the reply. "Team comms isolated, Sarge. What's going on?"

"I've got a feeling we're in for some serious shit from that HV."

To give him credit, he asked nothing more. My HUD flickered, the tac-map changing our five blue markers to green and picking out detail from the transport as the rest of the squad sent back enhanced scans of what we were heading towards.

"Hell, they've got a full platoon of armour on board, all suited and booted, and their gunners are all combat-ready," Reaper said. "Shouldn't someone tell them we're on the same side?"

Multiple scenarios ran through my head. "Everybody stay calm. We're all one big, happy family, and that's how we'll act until something changes. Angel, relay our thanks for the extract and give them our ETA."

"Roger that."

"Okay, squad; if this goes south, you know what to do. Ash, mask our systems, but show them our weapons going passive within a hundred metres. Everyone else, keep an eye out for cover, but play it cool."

* * *

We rounded a rocky outcrop to find the transport on the ground. The four massive rotors were still spinning, holding her at station, ready to dust off at a moment's notice.

It wasn't unusual in a combat zone, but the armoured troops trying too hard to act casual was. Eight of them, a long squad, stood on the loading ramp with an officer swathed in red and black: Military Intelligence.

Shit, I hated this crap. There had been a few exceptions in

my time, but on the whole, MI officers were stuffed too tight up their own assholes. I'd never liked them – not sure why. Maybe they just bred them like that through training. As a captain, he outranked me. Spec Ops got a little leeway, but I could tell it wasn't worth pushing it with this guy.

He looked down his nose at us, eyes flicking to the girl in my arms. "That's the asset?"

"I don't know if she's an asset, but this is the package we retrieved, sir."

"Hmm. Send her over here."

I lowered the kid to her feet, but she clung to my arm, hiding behind the leg of my armour. "That might be tricky, sir. As you can see, she's traumatised by what she's been through."

"My doctors will examine and tend to her needs."

I held tight as she tried to pull further away from the man, turning to face her. "It's okay. Nobody's gonna hurt you. I won't let them."

The frantic tugging to free herself lessened, but her wide eyes still carried a harrowed look as she peered past at the officer and his squad of goons.

"You seem to have made some connection with her – perhaps you should bring her over here?"

I turned back to the captain. "Aren't we just going to embark and get the hell out of here, before we catch any trouble from the locals, sir?"

His eyes didn't glass over, but the subtle movement in his jaw meant he was subvocalising commands.

"Did you get any of that, Ash?" I said, over our secure network.

"It's heavily encrypted, but local traffic. I'd guess he's talking with his meatheads. Give me a second."

"Will they notice?"

Ash laughed. "Unlikely."

The officer took a step forward. "We need to assess the asset first. Ensure it is the correct one, then we'll be leaving. If it is not, you'll receive additional orders."

I shook my head. "That's not how we work, sir. If you get Major LaSalle on the horn, she'll tell you that herself."

His eyes tore into me. "LaSalle is no longer in command of your section, Sergeant. Bring the package to me, now!"

The armoured grunts were perking up, weapons moving from their sides, coming up to ready positions. My instincts screamed at me. This guy would frag us as soon as he got the girl.

"Sarge?" Ash said. "He sent go-codes. He's marked our squad as enemy combatants."

"Roger that. Wait for my signal." I raised my hand. "Okay, no need for any trouble, sir. I'm just following Company policy. If things have changed, then you are the ranking officer." I stepped forward, pulling the kid alongside me. Thankfully, she didn't resist, and we moved toward the gunship. "Weapons hot," I sent, and all hell broke loose as I grabbed the girl, rolling us behind a thick outcrop of rock.

A boiling ball of flame burst where the rear section of the HV joined the ramp. The explosion from Pitbull's missiles rent the air, waves of heat beating at my armour while I huddled over Twelve, shielding her body. The transport rang with heavy rounds hammering into the fuselage as the big fifties opened up, raking a line of destruction toward the remaining armoured figures. The blast had embedded two of them in the canyon wall, strips of molten metal peeling away from the dark smears within.

The others were taking cover and trying to return fire, but the officer was nowhere in sight as I scanned the area.

"Stay here," I shouted to the kid over the tumult of gunfire. I turned, drawing my sidearm and putting two shots into an armoured helmet, dropping the soldier from the ramp.

A sandstorm swirled around me as the rotors growled into full power, lifting the bird from the ground. "Jam the missile launch codes."

"Already on it," Ash replied, calm as ever.

Automatic rounds punched into my chest plate, tracking upwards, and forcing me back a few steps. My HUD screamed information as something snapped. Yellow warnings flashed, highlighting the left shoulder of my suit, the armour there now at 75% integrity.

The rest of the team were in cover, except Pitbull. He continued his rain of fire onto the ramp section, trying to keep the troops' heads down. The whistle of hundreds of rounds per second and the staccato beat as they hit the transport's hull sang out through the madness.

The bird was ten metres up and starting to bank, bringing its main weaponry to bear on us. It lurched as Angel landed a shot right on the reinforced plexiglass cockpit. I don't care how good a pilot you are, seeing high-calibre rounds hitting the clear glass inches in front of your face is enough to spook anyone.

"Watch your six, Sarge," Reaper's voice called, and I turned weapon bearing onto a soldier emerging through the settling dust cloud. I dropped to one knee, plugging him twice, his shots passing over my head as he fell.

The next thing I knew was the thunderous roar of point defence weapons from the HV. They spewed fragments of supersonic titanium, designed to shred hardened vehicles and armour, tracking Angel's escape. Rock exploded all around her as the rounds vapourised all they touched into sandy coloured dust clouds.

Other PDWs spat their fury at where Ash and Pitbull were seconds before. Even our BFU wasn't stupid enough to take on the gunship head-to-head and was now pinned behind a rocky pillar. Reports from the rest of the team flicked across my screen. Most showed minor damage, but Pitbull had taken a pounding with critical warnings from his main weaponry and armour.

I sent Reaper to check on him, hoping he could help the big guy, but it didn't look good.

"Ash, speak to me," I called. "Tell me you got something up your sleeve."

"Hold a second, things are cooking," he said. "Okay...and... Adios, Motherfuckers."

The gunship's weapons fell silent, and I laughed. "You eighty-sixed the PDWs?"

"Not quite; they'll reset soon, but I screwed their internal comms. They won't be able to coordinate their assault."

"That'll do," I replied. "Squad, prepare to concentrate fire on the cockpit – it's our only chance."

I received affirmatives from everyone, even Pitbull. Seemed Reaper had worked his magic again, well enough to get the big guy back in the fight. Then I did something really stupid. Pulling out of cover, I stepped forward into the dust bowl and started firing at the pilot of the behemoth above us.

* * *

Now, you might think that was heroic, but I was out of options. I positioned myself to draw the beast into my team's arc of fire. If we could somehow crack the cockpit, then we could take the fucker down. However, the military is good at protecting weak spots, and the combat plexiglass is vacuum grade. It's what they used to protect spacefaring pilots from meteor strikes and other fighter weaponry. So it was a million to one shot, and that was probably over-optimistic.

Seems I'd done enough to piss someone off on board. The

beast lumbered in the air, orienting on me, picking up speed. A tsunami of rock and sand exploded toward me as their PDWs tore up the landscape. I stood there, pistol aimed at the cockpit, willing my team the one in a million chance this might work, and I wouldn't die, blasted to vapour.

Streams of green fireworks danced across my HUD as the others opened fire. The assault transport lumbered on, unhindered, chewing up the rugged basin as the titanium shards flew.

A single round sheared my right leg off, flinging me like a rag doll into a rocky wall. I remember the searing pain and my display flooding with red. Alarms shrieked, and my body flopped onto the craggy surface, face up, which is how I saw my last sight of the HV as it banked around for a second pass. Fragments of my shattered lower leg sparked as circuitry shorted against the metal frame, still trying to react to impulses from my struggling central processor.

There was no pain now, but my vision swam, and my systems were all over the place. My HUD flickered like some disco strobe, the approaching juggernaut, caught in slo-mo, as its magnetic accelerated rounds hurtled toward me. More green streams of fire from my team, desperate, hoping for a miracle that would save us all.

As my hearing faded, a shadow crossed my line of sight. A prolonged scream, anguish in the sound of a young girl's voice rent the air, then darkness.

* * *

PRIMARY BOOT SEQUENCE FAILED: FILES CORRUPT
IMPROPER SHUTDOWN DETECTED
REROUTING THROUGH SECONDARY BOOT CONTROLLER ...
... ... **COMPLETE**

SYSTEM DIAGNOSTIC
OPERATING INTEGRITY: 12%
BATTERY CAPACITY: 56%
CPU: 43%
STORAGE: 76%

REBUILDING MEMORY MATRIX FROM SECONDARY BACK-UP ... ...
WARNING: HARDWARE CORRUPTION — PERMANENT MEMORY FAILURE

SYSTEM ACTIVATING

Bright light streamed into darkness as I came back online. I was a mess, but somehow I'd survived. Streams of unknown code burst through my processor as systems reactivated.

"Hey, guess who's still hanging on in there?" Ash's voice sounded more relieved than I could ever have imagined.

"Where...am...I?"

"Try not to think too hard, Sarge. I've had to hack your secondary back-up to recover your memory. You've got some fatal hardware glitches, so some of it's gone for good, but that's a small price to pay for a second life, right?"

I said nothing. A strange, dull ache travelled throughout my body as I struggled to make sense of things. Thinking was slow and painful, leaving my brain feeling packed with cotton wool. On reflection, I'm not sure why that analogy came to me – my head was full of microcircuitry. All our heads were. Killer robots fucked over by their Human commanders. Maybe my systems glitched while Ash fought to save me, but I swore something cold touched my consciousness before I blacked out again.

A few reboots later, and things seemed a little clearer. My processor was back up to 74 percent, and I could think again.

The team gathered around me, telling how events had unfolded, and I watched the footage they'd captured of how Twelve had saved us all. A Human saving an Artificial, now go figure. Her scream of fear, rage, or whatever it was, had somehow emitted an enormous electromagnetic pulse that took down all the systems on the HV1, dropping it from the sky. It exploded like a supernova – the fact its missiles were armed must have had a lot to do with it – but we'd survived.

Feeling about as useful as a toaster, though, began wearing thin. The crash site was a molten waste of glass, with no chance for salvage, according to Reaper. He'd done what he could for me, welding a section of damaged armour to make a pegleg. I wobbled about like some fucking pirate captain, but he needed more raw materials or, better still, replacement parts and a workshop.

So, we were hiding out in a desert cave on a war-torn planet, trying to find a way out of this total Charlie-Foxtrot. The team were battered, and Pitbull grumbled about his lost toys, his missile array destroyed by the PDW fire. Its twisted frame now made up most of my new leg.

Other than being betrayed by our own side, and the fact we needed a route off this God forsaken rock, things weren't too bad. We were alive, and that's what mattered.

None of us had a clue what happened with Twelve; how she'd brought down a shielded behemoth like the HV1. She slept a lot and still didn't talk, but I owed her my life and that of the squad. Between us, we'd make sure we found her somewhere safe.

The bar stank of sweat and grease. Not unusual for a backwater system with no corporate interest. It was a dive like all the others on the sub-levels, full of ruthless people doing shady deals.

The boy across from me stared, eyes big as the moons of Celladon. I say 'boy', but he was probably in his early twenties, digital recorder forgotten on the cheap plastic table.

"So, you wanted the story of how Shadow Company formed, how the names you've heard about bonded into the most infamous mercenary unit in the core systems? Well, there you have it. Five old clankers and a mute kid called Twelve."

The youngster could have been a bot, the time he stared wide-eyed, jaw sagging under the weight of the artificial 1.2Gs. After what felt like an eternity, he blinked, proving he was a meatbag after all. "But she's a full-grown woman, and leader of your squad, isn't she?"

"Twelve? Yeah, I know she's not a kid anymore. But how she got to lead us? That's a whole different story."

GARETH CLEGG

Gareth lives in make-believe worlds somewhere in the dark spaces between science fiction, horror and fantasy. There he talks with imaginary friends and survives on a diet of tea, scones and the finest curries available to humanity.

His first novel - Fogbound: Empire in Flames - launched on Amazon on 8th Aug 2019 where it rose to become a best seller in the Steampunk Genre. It follows the efforts of a brave group, thrust together to save the British Empire in the wake of the failed Martian invasion of 1895.

Hailing from Huddersfield, in the UK, he enjoys all forms of Speculative fiction. His current project is a series of Weird Western Horror novellas - Chronicles of the Fallen.

To discover more about Gareth and his work, check his Amazon author page **http://Author.to/garethclegg** or his Social Media channels below.

facebook.com/fogbound1899

twitter.com/fogbound1899

instagram.com/fogbound1899

INVASION OF THE GREY ONES

"A VICTORIAN PSYCHOLOGIST BECOMES
EMBROILED IN A HORRIFIC INCIDENT AT A
LONDON SANITORIUM."

IAN F WHITE

I was called to the asylum by the eminent Doctor Earnest Brownlow on the morning of January 21st, 1886.

Taking the train to Waterloo, I hailed a Hansom at the station, and eventually stepped down from the carriage before the six stark columns of Bethlam hospital. I checked my pocket watch. It was five minutes past midday.

After paying the cabby his dues, I proceeded up the half-dozen steps and entered the lobby. I was immediately greeted by two gentlemen, the shorter - and more smartly attired - of whom introduced himself as Mister Davis, Doctor Brownlow's secretary.

I handed my hat, gloves and overcoat to the other man - Christianson, an orderly - and was led at a brisk pace to the good doctor's office.

Brownlow was in a flustered mood and barely acknowledged my arrival. Apparently there had been a number of unprecedented incidents of late and he was hard-pressed to resolve them. It soon transpired that I had been recruited to observe the perpetrator of one such incident; a certain Mister Charles Daventry.

Daventry had until recently been a compliant patient. However, two days prior to my visit, his violent nature had emerged. In the course of his restraint, two orderlies had been treated for fractures to the occipital and ulna bones respectively. He was currently in a semi-sedated state and, being a practising psychologist, I was asked to conduct enquiries.

I eagerly agreed and soon found myself seated upon a rickety wooden chair at the side of Daventry's bed, upon which he was - a burly and hirsute orderly assured me - firmly restrained.

Charles Daventry appeared to be in his late forties, as was suggested by his weather-beaten face, greying shoulder-length hair and unkempt beard, although his eyes - which opened as I entered the room - exhibited the extensive experience of a much older man.

"Good afternoon, Mister Daventry," I offered, smiling down at him.

He readily returned my smile, and I could see there were a few gaps in his amused grin. "Run," he advised me, "Flee, hide, while you have the chance."

"And why should I run?" I asked, maintaining my reassuring smile.

"They're coming."

I was definitely intrigued, although in hindsight, I should immediately have done as he suggested. "Who? Who are coming?"

"The Grey Ones, the ones from beyond the veil. It is they who are coming." His grin parted and he laughed maniacally for what seemed a full minute. I remained patient and eventually his laughter subsided but was immediately replaced by an alarming bout of coughing.

When that too had ebbed away, he stared at me with the assured sobriety of a holy man. "I am one of the few they chose. We are their mortal channels, the bridges by which they will cross from their world to ours."

I crossed one leg over the other and spent a moment smoothing away the creases on my trousers as I contemplated him. I then took out my pocketbook and a recently sharpened pencil and my examination began in earnest.

Despite having previously described his laughter as maniacal, as we talked, it dawned upon me that he was almost totally compos mentis although a little obsessed and fortunately easily guided in our conversation.

Over the course of the next half an hour, I filled a couple of pages in my pocketbook, scribbling down observations and considerations to research upon my return to my chambers in

Oxford Street. The burly orderly soon lost interest and entertained himself by staring out of the barred window.

The gist of what Daventry told me revolved around his extensive studies in the science of Astronomy and its related art of Astrology – in which, incidentally, so many of London's elite had recently become obsessively engrossed. That, in itself was not unusual for a college-educated and learned man, which I presumed Daventry to have been before his admittal. However, I must admit to being taken aback by his next - and quite disturbing - revelation.

The unprecedented incident eluded to by Doctor Brownlow concerned Daventry and another inmate, a man by the name of Fullerton. Apparently, the two men had indulged themselves in homosexual activity during their luncheon break in the main cafeteria. They had kissed in full view of staff and been quickly restrained and sedated in their respective rooms, not before rendering grievous bodily harm upon a number of unfortunate orderlies.

Daventry freely admitted to this unwholesome act, even going so far as to suggest that I should partake of an embrace myself, as it would hasten the arrival of his masters and perhaps afford me a level of protection, and a prime position in the new order that would follow their ascension.

I obviously declined and was about to end our conversation when he took a turn for the worse, suddenly affected by convulsive spasms that shook his whole body.

The springs of the bed frame twanged and creaked in objection as he arched his back one moment, only to bend the other way the next, in an attempt to sit upright. His restraints held him secure, although I could see how they dug savagely into his chafed bare flesh at wrist and neck.

"What's going on?" the orderly demanded, turning from the

window and frowning down upon Daventry's convulsing form. "Is he having a turn?"

"Yes," I replied, getting quickly to my feet, the notebook and pencil falling with a clatter to the bare floor. "He's going to hurt himself. Find a doctor; I'll hold him down."

The big man looked at me, obviously assessing my suitability for the latter task, and shook his head. He jabbed a stubby finger at me. "You go for a doctor... I'll hold him down."

"Very well," I quickly agreed and turned to the door.

I had only taken a single step when I recalled that the orderly had locked the sturdy wooden door behind us. I turned back to him, about to speak, and instinctively caught the ring of keys he flung at me. "It's number eight," he said.

I fumbled a moment with the unwieldy collection of ironmongery in my hands before locating the key etched with a number eight. One part of my slightly panicked mind registered that it resembled the symbol universally used to represent infinity. That brought a rueful twitch to my mustachioed lip.

With an enforced calmness, I inserted the key into the lock and twisted. The latch turned easily, rewarding my endeavor with a satisfying 'click'. Taking a quick look over my shoulder at the orderly, who was by now, almost lying fully atop the fitting Daventry in a seemingly futile attempt to hold him steady, I pulled the door open.

The door swung open on well-oiled hinges and I stepped out into the empty hallway.

My ears were immediately assailed by a cacophony of screams and yells of panic, seemingly emanating from both directions of the corridor. I was, again, momentarily stunned.

A door slammed loudly from further up the corridor and I instinctively looked in that direction. From my position, I could see the white strip of paper held in the brass mount screwed to the door, and name printed upon it. It read: JOSEPH FULLERTON.

As I stared, an orderly crawled out of the room, as if through a cloying mire; slow and deliberate. Even in his state, I recognised him as Christianson, the man who had taken my coat and hat. Blood dribbled from his mouth; lips drawn back in a feral grimace. I watched in stunned disbelief as he pulled himself clear of the door with red streaked hands. He dragged a steaming trail of intestines behind him for there was nothing left of him from the waist down. He saw me, opened his mouth and screamed "Help me!"

I knew there was nothing I could do for the man, yet I made as if to rush to his aid. My motion was halted as someone - *something* - else appeared in the doorway.

It was humanoid in shape and size, yet its skin was of a pale grey hue, glistening wetly in the harsh yellow light of the hallway bulbs. Its head was large for the body, the huge unblinking black eyes even more so. Blood dripped from its mouth and I caught a glimpse of fangs. Not teeth, but fangs. The long, spindly bare arms ended in claws, which clenched tightly upon the orderly's entrails like reins. It saw me too, but it did not scream, it simply grinned at me; an evil grin which turned my blood to ice.

I staggered backwards under its baleful gaze and came to an abrupt halt. Glancing fearfully over my shoulder, I realised I had stumbled into the orderly who had been restraining Daventry. I had not been given the man's name, and in some ways I was glad. He stared back at me, his face ashen, eyes bulging, almost pleading.

I tried to speak, but my throat was dry. I tried again, but the words emerged as a high-pitched scream - which I did not recognise as my own ululation - as a fist exploded from the orderly's chest. I was drenched in warm, wet, sticky fluid. I wiped a hand over my face and stared into the dead eyes of the orderly.

His lifeless legs gave way and he sagged, supported only by whatever had killed him. The grey hand was withdrawn and the dead man slid to the blood-soaked, tiled floor with a wet, soggy splat.

The creature now revealed was similar to the one behind me, yet as I stared in dumbfounded terror into the face which framed those mesmerizing black orbs, I saw a resemblance to the man I had been speaking to a mere five minutes previously. It was Charles Daventry!

"My God," I managed to utter, my voice a croaky whisper, which seemed so loud in the now silent corridor.

Daventry grinned. "Indeed..." he said. But the hellish voice did not assail my ears; it was in my mind, in my very soul. "I am your God."

"No!" I yelled and leapt aside.

My left shoe slipped in the orderly's freshly spilled blood and I lost my balance, arms flailing wildly. That was what saved my life.

Daventry's clawed hand raked along my cheek, but that was much more desirable than the potential alternative. I squealed in pain, ducked low and sprinted down the hallway.

The two Grey Ones did not pursue, they merely laughed: a sickly, cloying laugh which coated the walls of my mind with thick grey ichor.

My mad dash out of that demon haunted asylum was short, yet each step was filled with horror. I saw more of the creatures, dismembering the inmates and employees whom they had not chosen as their bridges. I stumbled through the remains of orderlies and nurses, past blood-soaked rooms, I saw the decapitated heads of Davies and Brownlow in the main hall and then I finally stumbled out into the harsh daylight.

I blinked in the golden glare and paused.

But as I did so, the laughter began again.

I ran for my life, without regard for social decency, through the gas-lit streets of the city, ignoring all who threw questioning glances and curses in the wake of my blind flight. I ran until I could run no more, until my lungs burned for want of oxygen, until my legs were as jelly. I ran until I found a dark place in which to hide, in which to turn my back upon the horror I had witnessed, yet could scarce believe was true.

And now, here I am, huddled in the corner of my cellar, the salty taste of tears and iron of blood upon my lips, the unforgettable sound of Daventry's mocking laughter in my mind, the images of dismembered bodies indelibly etched on my retina, listening to the pitiful screams of the victims of the invasion of the Grey Ones.

IAN F WHITE

Ian F White has been sharing his story-telling creations since the mid-1980s, initially in the form of roleplaying and wargaming scenarios, but more recently as regular literary work. He currently has more than ten titles available, mostly concerning the Action & Adventure genre with occasional jaunts into Horror, Fantasy, Science-Fiction, and Comedy.

He lives in Huddersfield, West Yorkshire, with his mutually devoted wife, and cats.

You can find out more at his
    Amazon Author's Page: **author.to/Ian-F-White**
    or on his Website **https://wyvernebg.webs.com/**

CHILDREN OF THE NIGHT

"A RACE OF SHADOW PEOPLE CLASHES
WITH THE WORLD OF MEN IN AN EFFORT
TO SAVE THE NIGHT FROM LIGHT
POLLUTION."

NICK STEAD

Hear me. In the chirping of crickets and the roaring of the great cats stalking my twilight plains, the howling of coyotes and the hooting of the owls watching in the trees above, and in the croaking of the frogs and toads calling for a mate, hear my song. I live in every creature roaming the hours of darkness, every plant who blooms not for the harsh light of the sun but for the softer glow of my beloved moon, and in the moon itself. More than that, I live in the stars, and the sky they reside in. For I am the Night and my voices are many, my song endless.

But my song is changing. It began with the rise of the race of men, children of the Day driven by selfishness and greed. They learnt to take what they want from the land around them and shape it to their advantage, but in their greed, they lost sight of all that was once sacred. They have no thought for all that is natural and the harm they cause to other living beings. They are not troubled by the irreparable damage they do to this beautiful planet, nor do they show any interest in preserving the delicate balance our world hangs in, not even for future generations who will surely suffer as many creatures have suffered already. No, they care only for themselves and their society. And it is all other lifeforms who must pay the price.

Now my song is becoming the thumping drumbeat of club music, the roaring of car engines, and the shouts and drunken laughter of this race which never sleeps. Yet of all the destruction mankind has wrought upon this earth, it is their love of light which hurts me most. A love that began with the discovery of how to make fire, and which ends with this artificial glow now conquering my twilight realm. A glow which disrupts my children and blinds and disorientates, upsetting the harmony that once existed between myself and my daytime counterparts.

My song is changing, but the voices of my children remain, for those who care to listen. So hear me. Hear my pain as I am wounded over and over by millions of light shafts not just stabbing and piercing, but seeking to drive me back in favour of eternal day. Hear my sorrow as my children struggle on in conditions they are not suited for, and watch me weep for all those who die needlessly, all for mankind's selfishness. For I am the Night and I am dying, and my song is no longer endless.

* * *

Such was the story told by Torik's people. He was only young when he heard it for the first time, under a new moon when the Night was at her strongest. Even then there'd been the invasive light emanating from the world of men, brightening the horizon with its unwelcome and unnatural glow. The sight of it already played on his childhood fears, but he felt something new rising in him at the nightsinger's words. It was an emotion he was too young to know well, for he had been lucky to not yet have been touched by grief. But he did hear the Night's sorrow as she spoke through her chosen vessel and he felt it within him, though he had no tears to shed.

Something was awoken in Torik that night. The words resonated deep in his heart and continued to echo around his head for many hours after the nightsinger had fallen silent. He'd been full of questions afterwards, questions his parents couldn't answer. Only the nightsinger could speak with the voice of Mother Twilight, and in their clan that was Alina. But Alina was old and fading, spending more and more time alone in her cave with each passing decade. There she seemed to sleep mostly, in between communing with their Mother.

It was under that same new moon that his vision came. Dawn was almost upon them and they had retreated into their own caves when the comforting darkness slipped away from Torik and a bright glare slid over his eyes, tainting his sight and limiting all he should have been able to see of the world. Perhaps it was a blessing he found himself blinded, because in that fluorescent haze there was only horror.

The sky was gone. There was only the glare, obscuring the moon and the stars which had been a part of his life from the moment he'd first opened his eyes. Without them there was no sense of place or direction. There was nothing to guide him back to the shadows where he belonged, and it was not just he who was lost.

Birds flew by the millions into man's towering structures and fell in a feathery hail, littering the ground with their broken, lifeless bodies. Prey stood exposed to predator and died one by one, until there was nothing left but bloody bones. Some predators enjoyed a period of plentiful hunting and were free of hunger for a time, yet as Torik watched, the numbers of prey started to dwindle, and the predators with them.

Other predators faded much quicker without the cover of darkness they'd relied on to stalk the creatures whose flesh nourished them. Lions and other majestic beasts wasted away, the twilight plains once so rich with life now turning to a wasteland realm of death and decay.

Torik looked out over that wasteland and witnessed the end. It was chaos, and it affected the children of the Day as well. For man's unnatural lights were disruptive to the countless creatures relying on the patterns of night and day changing with every season, and mating rituals were beginning too early or too late, the young born into harsh conditions they could not survive. The Night had died, and the Day was soon to follow her.

Torik returned to the present, screaming with both horror and his first taste of grief, more profound even than the sorrow he'd felt at Alina's words. Somewhere outside of that horror a voice spoke, and Torik's destiny took shape.

"He is the one," Alina said. It seemed she'd risked crossing through the Day's banishing rays to enter their cave so she could investigate the source of his screams. "He will lead us in the great war to come, and together we will restore Mother Twilight to her former glory."

* * *

So there he was, fully grown and warlord of his clan in the fight to save the planet against an enemy who did not even know they were at war. But war was not his only calling.

Torik alone could walk among their daytime cousins, gifted the power to take human shape – a power discovered in the nights following his vision. As flesh and blood, he was able to pass beneath the light without fear of eternal banishment, and he had been tasked with the responsibility of first attempting to reason with mankind and open their eyes to the damage they wrought on the land. The nightsingers maintained it was their Mother's wish to avoid war if possible, for enough lives had been lost on man's count. And so he must first seek a peaceful resolution before leading his people into battle.

Leaving the darkness of the wilderness he'd always called home and venturing into the human world was perhaps the most terrifying experience of his life, save for the vision which had set him on this fateful path. It was made all the harder by the fact it was a solitary path. His clan followed him to the very edge of the glow surrounding the city he must enter, but they could go no further. He wanted nothing more than to turn back with them and spend the rest of the night as they had always done, caring for Mother Twilight in all her guises and telling her story, but that was not his destiny. So he let his shadow self solidify into flesh and bone and fashioned clothes from the darkness around him, stepping under the light as a human.

Never had he felt so alone. The stars he knew so well were no longer visible beneath the glare of the lights assaulting his eyes from every angle. As a man his vision had an easier time of adjusting to it than in his true form, yet that did nothing to lessen his discomfort. He felt lost without either the comfort of his clan around him or the stars overhead to guide him on his journey. His entire being yearned to return to the darkness where he belonged, and it took all his willpower to keep himself moving further into the city.

"Mother, give me strength," he muttered. Her answer came in the chuckling of a hyena, somewhere out on the plains, and brought the courage needed to go on.

Torik had not been walking the city streets for long when his eyes fell on a rough-looking bar, uninviting to most but full of promise for one such as he. The interior looked to be dingy enough to offer some comfort, even if it was not the beauty of the night he was used to. And there were bound to be humans inside.

"What'll it be?" the barman asked as Torik ventured in and tentatively made his way over.

Torik just looked at him. The words were different to the language of his people but it seemed his gift had given him an understanding of the human tongue, and the ability to speak it as well as his own.

A moth fluttered by, distracting him from the barman. She was a welcome sight in unfamiliar territory, and he followed her over to one of the tables by the wall where she became more frenzied in her flight, mesmerised by the dull glow of the lamp hanging there. Torik was as transfixed by her as she was by that dim bulb, and he didn't notice the human sat nearby until the man took a drinks menu and swatted at the insect.

"What are you attacking for?" Torik asked, horrified by the human's actions.

"I can't stand bugs," the man answered. "They've always given me the creeps."

The moth had barely escaped the menu. She would have been swatted a second time but Torik grabbed the man's arm before he could strike, holding him back.

"She isn't doing you any harm. What gives you the right to kill her, just because you find her repulsive? Does she not have the same right to life as you?"

"How do you know it's a she?" the man asked, pulling free of his grip.

"Because she is a child of the Night, and I know all of the Night's creatures."

The man frowned at him, apparently not sure what to make of that. "I think you might have been at the ale for too long tonight, friend. Can I call you a taxi home to sleep it off?"

"Ale?" Torik asked, confused. In his natural state he had no need of food or drink.

"Wow, you must be drunk. You know, beer, lager. Let's get you outside at least – maybe the fresh air will do you some good."

"Yes, outside would be good. I am not as comfortable in here as I thought I'd be, despite the darkness of this interior."

The man laughed. "Whatever you say, dude. I'm Luke, by the way."

"Torik," he answered, following Luke out. The barman scowled as they passed. Torik recognised the expression as a display of aggression, though he was not sure what he'd done to upset this other human. He was still puzzling over it when they emerged back onto the street, the night sky overhead both comforting and depressing.

"What is it?" Luke asked, raising his own eyes to the sky.

"Hmm? Oh, nothing. I was just looking for the stars."

"I never saw the fascination myself. It always felt cold and empty up there to me."

"No! There is beauty up there; you just can't see it for all this artificial lighting." A thought took shape in Torik's mind. He'd been tasked with teaching humans the error of their ways, and perhaps this man was to be the first. "Let me show you."

"I don't know, it's late and the wife's waiting for me back home. Maybe another time?"

"It won't take long," Torik answered, beginning to feel more sure of himself. If he could win this man over, perhaps he could gain an ally to help spread the word amongst other children of the Day. "Come, let me show you."

"What the hell, I'm all for trying new things. Prove me wrong and I'll buy you a drink next time I see you."

Torik smiled and led Luke back towards the wilderness. But when they reached the city's edge, Luke came to a stop and shook his head, his eyes widening in fear.

"Oh no, I'm not going out there," the human said.

"Why not?"

"It's not safe at night, everyone knows that. The darkness is full of dangerous animals, and thieves and murderers." Luke's eyes widened further, his features settling into a look of pure horror. "Wait, is that what this is? You want to drag me out there so you can kill me and leave me to rot?"

"I have not come to kill anybody. I merely wish to share the night's beauty with your people, if you will let me. Please, we need not go far. Just a little way out of the light so you can see for yourself what lies beyond."

"Forget it, I'm not going wandering off into the night with some guy I only just met. It's time I was getting a taxi home and I suggest you do the same."

Torik looked on in despair as the man stormed off. Reasoning with them seemed impossible when their fear of the darkness appeared to be so deeply ingrained in the human psyche, and yet he could not just give up after one unsuccessful encounter. He would report back to his people before the dawn forced them to take shelter from the sun, but he would be back the next night and the night after that, for as long as it took to persuade them the Night was not their enemy. Perhaps it was hopeless, but he had to try.

* * *

And so Torik spent his nights, learning all he could of the human world and teaching them of his. He crossed paths with Luke many times, and after a while they formed an unlikely friendship, growing so close that they were no longer cousins but brothers.

Once he had his brother's trust, Torik tried again to show his friend the beauty he was missing, and finally Luke agreed. Together they went into the darkness, and together they gazed on the night sky with awe.

"See what your people are missing out on?" Torik said. "If you could just turn off some of your lights, we would all benefit from Mother Twilight's beauty shining over us."

"You keep saying 'your people' like you're different from us. Are they not your people too?"

"Perhaps a part of me is becoming one with your world, but I can never truly belong to human society so long as you insist on keeping Mother Twilight out. In my heart I will always be a child of the Night."

"I've no idea what any of that means, but for some reason I love you anyway. I think you must be infecting me with your madness, bro," Luke laughed.

There was a rustling in the grass around them and the human's laughter died in his throat.

"What was that?" Luke asked, digging in his pocket for his phone. The Night retreated before the bright light it emitted, stumbling back a few steps. It was enough to bring the human comfort.

But Torik felt another wave of despair at seeing his friend's fear. Just when he thought they'd been making progress the human had fallen back into his misguided beliefs about the nature of the Night. Teaching them did not appear to be working, and war seemed inevitable.

* * *

Torik returned to his people, heartbroken and near defeated. He told them of this latest turn of events, and all shared in his despair.

"Then we have no other choice," Alina spoke up. Her shape had all but collapsed, soon to become one with the darkness again. It was a wonder she'd lasted so long as it was. They expected her to return to their Mother any night now, when a new nightsinger would be chosen to take her place. "It can only be war."

Torik had been dreading this night for some time. He was not violent by nature, and once he had overcome his fears of the city lights, he had come to favour the peaceful attempts to save their world. He'd agreed with the nightsingers that mankind had been the cause of enough deaths, and he had no appetite for bloodshed, not even when it was the blood of humans he'd be spilling. But he could not deny the truth of Alina's words. It seemed they had no other choice.

The raids began on the city in the nights that followed. At first, he sought only to break the lights and pave the way for his people to enter the streets, so that they might damage the electrics powering the city and let the Night return to the human world. He was determined only to kill humans if they gave him no other option, and he demanded the other warriors with him do the same. But such measures could only bring small and temporary victories. For every night spent reclaiming one area of the city, there were the daylight hours in which the humans worked to repair the damage and the light returned. And the world was now so full of humans, it would take the Myrkur years to put out every single light that had sprung up on the planet. Once again, the situation seemed hopeless.

A warrior by the name of Oru approached him one night, not long after dusk while they were preparing for another raid.

"Forgive me, Lord, but I feel I must point out to you that which you surely know for yourself – this isn't working. Mankind will never change. We should be extinguishing them, and only then will their lights follow into the abyss. It is the only way this war can be won."

"I hear you, Oru, but what you talk of is genocide. I won't wipe humanity off the face of the planet. There is goodness in them and there are some who are beginning to understand the damage they are causing, and are working to undo it. We just need the majority to see it."

"And how long will that take? Our Mother does not have enough years left in her to wait for humanity to fix the problems they're creating. You are our warlord, Mother Twilight's champion – saviour of the Night. You can't keep avoiding your responsibilities. It's time to make the hard choices she has entrusted to you, or we must surely perish."

"I'm not avoiding anything," Torik said, anger rising in him. "But I will not take the lives of humans who remain innocent. Don't you see? My time among them has taught me they are not all to blame, and if we kill them all then how are we any better than they?"

"You cannot fight a war while you still have ties to both sides.

It is time you gave up your human body and returned wholly to our people, so you can become the leader you were chosen by the Mother herself to be. I will say no more. Think on my words, and for our Mother's sake I hope you will do what is right."

But what was right? Torik could not bring himself to be a part of the slaughter of billions, and yet in killing those billions would he not be saving billions more and rescuing countless species from the suffering they were currently trapped in under mankind's reign? It was a hard choice, and one without any clear solutions.

* * *

The raid that night did not go to plan, and the war finally turned bloody.

It started with the grand opening of the new stadium they'd managed to delay, but not completely stop. Floodlights lanced through the darkness, piercing with their intense beams and making the Night scream louder than ever before.

The new light confused migrating birds and they smashed into buildings. Feathered bodies rained down just as Torik had seen in his vision all those years ago. Their corpses crashed to the ground where they lay in crumpled heaps, broken and lifeless. Was this the beginning of the end he had foreseen?

Torik and his clan fought back, attacking the unnatural light with spears of shadow and swords of moonlight, but Oru was right: as long as mankind lived, their lights would live on with them, no matter how many times they were extinguished and relit. Yet still he was reluctant to shed more blood.

Then came the thing he'd feared most since first leading his people into battle. For Oru had also been right in that he had ties to the humans as well as his own race. Namely Luke, his brother, who he had not seen in several months. Not since that night they'd shared in the beauty of the stars, for he'd avoided all contact with the human world after that. Except for the deliberate clashes during the fighting, of course, but he'd been careful not to hit the parts of the city which he knew his brother to frequent. And by avoiding those areas, he'd been successful in keeping Luke out of it. Until now.

He stared across the battlefield in horror, fearing for his friend's safety. But there was no recognition on Luke's face. How could there be? Torik was fighting as his true shadow self, not the man Luke had come to know.

The humans turned their lights on Torik and his warriors and several of them were caught in the beams. Their screams were cut short with a terrible finality as they simply ceased to be, winking out of existence without leaving any trace they had ever been. Banished from the earth, they would never be allowed to re-join the darkness of their Mother like those who met a natural end, nor would they ever have the chance to be reborn as new shadows cast by the soothing light of the moon. It was a fate worse than death.

Oru took matters into his own hands then, hacking and slashing at their daytime cousins as well as the unnatural lights. More bodies fell, the street now running red with blood.

Luke watched all this with wide eyes, unable to comprehend what was really going on. The man panicked when the Myrkur succeeded in killing all lights in the immediate vicinity, running for the street lamps shining only a handful of streets away. Torik realised the danger his friend was in and ran after him.

Luke made it to the nearest brightly lit street, but Torik's fear only grew at the sight of his friend standing exposed in the light, just like the other prey he'd seen in his vision. Shifting into his flesh and blood human self, Torik yelled to his brother, but he was too late. He could only watch in horror as a hungry panther burst from the shadows at the end of the street. The beast leapt and sank her fangs into his brother's neck. Luke fell beneath the predator, his shock plastered across his face.

The irony was not lost on Torik as he stood in shock himself, watching the blood running down the pavement and dripping into the gutter. Luke had been so afraid of the dangers lurking in the darkness that he had initially refused to enter it to see the stars, placing such faith in the city lights to keep him safe.

But ultimately those lights had been his undoing, as they would be the undoing of all mankind. For it was the light which had marked him out as the perfect prey for the panther, and so she'd seized the opportunity and attacked. Had he stayed under the cover of darkness, he might have gone unnoticed by the night's predators and he would still be alive, perhaps dreaming of the stars his strange friend had shown him and puzzling over all the secrets his friend undoubtedly had. But he had not, and so his misguided belief had cost him his life.

Grief ripped its way through the shock and erupted from Torik in a scream. "Luke!"

The panther raised her head and gave a startled cry. She took up a defensive stance, snarling a warning. But Torik paid it no heed. He ran to his friend, brandishing his sword at the panther and screaming again to drive her away. She turned tail and ran.

Torik fell to his knees and cradled Luke's head, roaring his pain for all the night to hear. Tears streamed from his eyes and new despair seized his heart.

He wanted to believe there was still hope for the planet, that he and his people might someday succeed in turning humanity from their destructive ways and restoring the harmony that once existed between human civilisation and the natural world, the sun and the moon, and Day and Night. But he feared the worst.

The Night is dying, her time is running out, and her song is no longer endless.

NICK STEAD

A lifelong fan of supernatural horror and fantasy, Nick spends his days prowling the darker side of fiction, often to the scream of heavy metal guitars and the purrs of his feline companions. Werewolves are his speciality but only the monstrous kind – you won't find any tame puppies in this author's works!

Fate set him on the path of the writer at the tender age of 15. The journey has been much longer and harder than his teenage self ever anticipated, but 17 years later he is still forging ahead.

Nick is best known for his Hybrid series. He has also had short stories published in various anthologies, and will soon be releasing his first non-Hybrid novel based on the true story of the Pendle witches.

How to find Nick
   Web: Nick-Stead.co.uk
   Amazon Author Page: author.to/nickstead
   Or follow his Social Media channels below

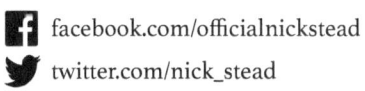

   facebook.com/officialnickstead
   twitter.com/nick_stead

THE LOVERS OF ODFELLOW LANE

"A WOMANIZER COMES BETWEEN TWO CUNNING WOMEN."

OWEN TOWNEND

It had never occurred to Thomas that Belle would stick around for so long. He was used to his relationships only lasting a week or so. And yet he had been with her for almost a month now. He struggled to understand it.

"You're not my first commitment-phobe," she spoke up.

Thomas flinched. He hadn't actually said a word about this to her. "What?"

Belle chuckled. "I could read the panic on your face."

He squirmed in her bedsheets. "That's really not it."

"Don't deny it," she said, patting him on his hairy chest. "I know the type."

"And what happened to them?"

Belle evaded this question by pulling him in close. Thomas certainly admired the way she wound herself around him. He enjoyed the strange rainbow sheen of her raven hair whenever she moved nearer. Even so, was this love? He couldn't tell.

And yet, six days out of seven Thomas was up at her cluttered apartment on Odfellow Lane. Her bed was ridiculously comfortable with its silken sheets and perfumed pillows. And there was the way she stretched when she climbed out: her thin wrists joining above her head, the slight curve to her pale chin disappearing in a puppy dog yawn. Belle frowned at her rustic bronze alarm clock.

"Shit," she said. "My appointment."

Thomas sat up, enjoying the static of his toes against the mattress. "Dentist? Doctor? Optician?"

"Therapy," she replied, stumbling into her raggedy jeans as she hopped across the hardwood floor. The vibration sent some loose papers flying off the top of her antique mahogany bureau. "Shitty shit shit!"

"Head shrinking? Kudos. Not something I'd put myself through."

Having thrown on her silver blouse, Belle glared at him. "Be thankful."

It was Thomas' turn to stretch. "I always am."

She climbed across the bed and kissed him. "Don't leave until Pittance feeds you."

"Is she here?"

"She's usually around."

"If Pittance is such a homebody then how come she has more of a tan than you?"

Belle shared a conspiratorial wink. "Would you believe it's spray-on?"

"Surely not."

"Neither of us do well in direct sunlight." Belle stepped into some well-worn black trainers. "Now really, I've got to go."

"Of course," Thomas said, yawning. "Hope therapy goes well. Try not to question your current life choices too much."

"Everything comes under the microscope sometime or another."

Belle left with a cheeky grin that Thomas couldn't quite read. Normally simple cuteness didn't appeal to him for long but, with Belle, there seemed more to it than that. Being with her felt like he was speaking with an alluring voice at the opposite end of a long tunnel. The voice might know him well, be keen to play, but then, why was it waiting? Why didn't it meet him halfway?

Thomas shook off such dreamy thinking, dressed himself and descended the stairs. He found Pittance in the kitchen with her back turned to him. Slight clinking suggested she was counting money again. Always pennies and without explanation.

At last she turned to him, her long grey doily cardigan swishing open. She had a much bigger face than Belle with brown eyes peering out through a mane of black curls. Pittance seemed so unnatural in everything she did and yet she didn't seem to mind Thomas staring.

"Counting your wealth?" he asked.

"This?" Pittance shrugged, referring to the stacks of old copper coins she had laid on the granite countertop. "This is just change."

"A lot of change." There were a dozen piles of pennies, all the same height and perfectly neat. Thomas scrutinised them. "And here I was thinking Belle was the organised one."

"Nothing goes to waste around here." Pittance had an uneven smile. Some of her teeth were sharper than others, especially in the back. Still, if she brought her ruby red lips together, you would never know.

Thomas nodded towards the oven just to her left. "Anything on the go?"

Her eyes widened. "You're presumptuous."

"Blame Belle. She offered your services as a cook."

Pittance shrugged again. This time it was much slower and more exaggerated, like she was limbering up to something. "I could heat something up."

"Need assistance?"

She leant towards Thomas. Her hand moved behind him, cool skin lightly brushing his side. They locked eyes. He reminded himself of Belle. Thomas brought her face to mind, the unspoken commitment between them, the concept of his emotional growth as opposed to the other growth that was happening down below right now.

Pittance laughed in his face. She revealed a pan. "Eggs?" she asked.

"I can help with that," he said.

Thomas moved aside as Pittance reached for the egg box and switched on the stove.

"You know, you ought to be careful," she said.

"I have cracked eggs before."

Pittance shook her head. "I mean with Belle."

"I know," Thomas said, egg yolk slipping out between his fingers. "She is a wonderful person. I would never ever think of hurting her."

Pittance laughed again. It always began shrill before softening. "She could hurt you worse."

"Tell me about it." He winked. "I have claw marks on my back."

There was no laughter at this. "Does she ever ask you what's on your mind?"

Thomas frowned. "No, actually."

"And yet she seems to know anyway? To anticipate what you want to do next?"

"Sometimes, I suppose." Thomas cocked an eyebrow. "Mind you, she doesn't always deliver."

"Doesn't that bother you?"

"It bothers me tremendously."

Pittance fixed him with a stern look. "I'm saying that I know Belle is unusually perceptive."

"It's what makes her wonderful." Thomas turned to her. "Surely?"

Pittance just prodded the eggs with a spatula, their hiss steadily rising and filling up the kitchen. Some fat leapt out of the pan and made him flinch.

Eventually the eggs were fried enough to slip onto blue china plates. Thomas had got toast ready in the meantime. When he bit into his slice, Pittance spoke again. "I can help you."

"Help?"

She held his gaze. "I can protect your mind."

"From what? Belle?"

Pittance nodded. A loose strand of her hair flickered all

colours of the rainbow, just like with Belle. He hadn't noticed that before. "How?"

"I can break the hold she has on your thoughts."

Something about the way Pittance described this made Thomas take heed. Sometimes it did feel like Belle was in his head, that she was much more present than his past girlfriends had ever been. What he felt for her seemed like love but then it was surely too invasive to be simply that. Almost as if it had been forced upon him. Any chance he could get to put that into perspective was surely worth taking.

"Why?" he asked.

"Because I like you," Pittance said, moving closer again. "You're much too easy."

Thomas flinched. "I may have been around the block a few times but I do have my dignity."

Pittance's lips parted, showing teeth. "Dignity's usually the first to go," she whispered.

* * *

Sometime later, Thomas sat up in Pittance's bed. This hadn't been how he had planned his day but, all the same, he couldn't bring himself to leave now.

He stared ahead for the longest time, his brow stuck in a frown. This experience was nothing like it had been before. Not so long-ago, bed-hopping at lunchtime felt like an achievement of sorts. Then again, that was before Belle.

Belle with her kind green eyes set in a childish face. Belle with her uncanny knack for predicting just what he was about to say. Even if he didn't quite love her, at least he knew that she could make him feel guiltier than ever before.

Thomas's quiet focus was momentarily broken by a flash of Pittance in her bathroom, the door wide open. He opened his mouth to say something when Pittance walked out. She was wearing a baggy black shirt depicting the universe. Thomas found himself staring at the constellation above her knickers.

He pulled himself up short. Nevertheless, Pittance seemed mildly amused.

"You're feeling guilty."

"Careless too."

Pittance sighed. "Belle will definitely work out what we did if you keep pouting like that."

Thomas shut his eyes. He could already hear Belle screaming at him, the accusations that he couldn't deny. He had betrayed her trust.

"She's had much worse," Pittance replied. Thomas looked up. She had suggested that she could read him but then surely that was all banter. Foreplay. He touched his fingers to his forehead.

"Belle doesn't deserve an opportunist scumbag like me in her life," he said.

"She lets in who she lets in."

Thomas frowned again. "You really don't seem much of a friend, saying that."

Pittance shrugged and landed heavily against the headboard, beside him.

"My relationship with Belle is more like sisterhood."

"So, I'm the mister who comes between the sisters?" Thomas rolled his eyes. "Lord help me."

Pittance touched his face lightly. "You don't need the Lord for this. You just need me."

Thomas sighed. He looked straight at her. "And what can you do?"

"I can make you forget."

"Forget?"

"That this ever happened. That you cheated on Belle. That you ever gave in to your baser urges."

"Wouldn't that be nice?"

She didn't seem to hear the sarcasm in his tone. "I can clear the last two hours of your memory but leave you with the post-coital bliss."

"Quite the offer." He smiled. "I can't say I trust it coming from a woman who probably wouldn't want to be forgotten."

Pittance's eyes widened slightly but enough for Thomas to notice and shrink.

"I am never forgotten. I make people forget." She slowly softened. "Trust me. I know what I'm doing."

"You've done this before?"

"Yes."

"To Belle?"

Pittance didn't answer; instead, she reached behind her to her bedside drawer. A rainbow sheen arced down from her roots to her ends. She pulled out a handful of coins. Thomas could hear them rattling against one another. He couldn't look down though: his eyes were stuck, following Pittance's. She raised a penny into his tunnel vision, alongside a flat empty hand.

"One," she said, laying the coin on it.

A new coin appeared. "Two."

Thomas heard the coin scrape and clink against the other.

"Three," Pittance said, though Thomas did not hear this third coin.

Thomas heard nothing. He just blacked out.

Thomas awoke to a hiss. He gasped, glancing around him. He was in the kitchen, sat at the table. He was fully dressed. Of course he was dressed. Why wouldn't he be? Still, the white button-up shirt suddenly looked wrong on him. It was too clean and not at all crumpled.

The hiss got louder. His eyes settled on its source. Someone was frying eggs.

The woman's back was to him. He recognised the dark hair but he did not know who was on the other side of it. It seemed like it was Belle. And yet...

"Pittance?" he asked.

The woman turned. Of course, it wasn't Pittance. Belle was the short one. He blinked, wondering just how long his eyes would need to adjust.

She laughed at him. "What do you mean Pittance?"

"Pittance?" Thomas blinked. "I don't..."

Belle switched off the hob and moved over to him. Her fingers slid over his.

"What's up?" she asked. "Where's your head at?"

Thomas coughed up a little laugh of his own. "I honestly don't know. Must have been somewhere far away."

"You've been here all afternoon." Belle's tone was quiet but firm.

Thomas frowned at her. "But where is Pittance? Out of interest?"

"She left an hour ago. Said you had a phone call that kept you busy all this time." Belle frowned now. "Don't you remember?"

Thomas took a moment to search his memory. It made him wince.

"Something money-related," he muttered.

Belle nodded slowly. "It left you pretty distracted, she said."

Thomas tried again. His whole brain screamed. He clutched his temples.

Belle touched his face lightly. Something about this simple act caused his attention to focus directly on her eyes. They were shining with concern.

"That money," she said. "Could it have been Pittance's coins?"

Thomas sighed. "Could have been."

"I knew I shouldn't have believed her," she whispered, voice gradually buzzing with anger. Her hand pulled away. "I knew it."

Thomas opened his mouth but the words wouldn't come out straight away.

"Wh-what? What do you mean by that?"

Belle didn't say a word to him, though her hand remained hovering mid-air. Thomas didn't quite know why but he expected it to slap him.

Instead Belle stared at him, gently rubbing the curve of her chin with her forefinger, as if in thought. This went on a while. Clearly it meant something more but Thomas had no idea what. He was transfixed. He literally could not turn away from this simple, strange face touch. She turned her eyes on him.

Belle breathed in slowly through her button nose. She breathed out even slower through her puckered lips.

She inhaled slower. She exhaled even slower.

Belle inhaled a lifetime. Belle exhaled forever.

* * *

Thomas must have dozed off. He had no idea that he was so tired.

His eyes fell on Belle's bedside table. There was a lumpy purple stone in front of her alarm clock. He reached across and picked it up. He had never noticed it before, though there was plenty of dust around it. It was porous with a fold down the middle. It looked like a withered brain.

"Why do you keep doing this?" Belle spoke.

Thomas hurriedly put the stone back on the table before realising that she wasn't actually in the room with him. She sounded to be just outside.

"I'm sorry," Pittance replied, though she didn't actually sound apologetic, "They're just so predictable."

"Seriously, stay the fuck away from my boyfriends! And for God's sake, stop revealing what we can do!" A pause. "Why are you smiling like that?"

"What we can do," Pittance said, "is precisely what we do to them. Both of us."

"What you do to them is far crueller than anything I would!"

"And you seriously believe their own intentions are any better?" There was a sliver of ice to Pittance's tone here. "Always looking for something stranger. More...exotic."

"They may be weak-willed but you're worse! You should know better!"

"Are you going to tattle on me, Belle?"

"You're making it impossible not to."

"I don't think you will." Another pause. Pittance laughed, shriller than ever. "Just goes to show how much this one matters to you."

"He does," Belle replied, all the enthusiasm draining from her voice. "This one hurt, Pittance. Really hurt."

Another, much longer pause.

"Shit!" Pittance said. "Your boyfriend's awake!"

"He's still groggy."

"I can hear him shuffling about in there. His fidgety little thoughts..."

"Will you help me get him home, at least?"

"I'll certainly help you knock him out."

Thomas heard the distinct sound of coins clinking. It was oddly familiar and not at all welcome. The door opened. Belle stared at him from the doorway. At last, Thomas could see the full disappointment in her eyes.

"Belle!" he said. "I can explain..."

Pittance stood beside her with her sharp-tooth smile. The

black hair of both women suddenly shimmered every colour of the rainbow.

In a moment, all the light around them dimmed.

* * *

Thomas rose from his bed with a splitting headache. He checked the time: 3:45pm. Where had the day gone? It was like he was a student again.

He threw off his bed covers and found he was fully dressed. He tried to cast his mind back to the last thing he could remember. As he did this, he found himself moving into his kitchenette. He stopped at the stove. He reached for a pan, a vague memory of greasy fried eggs filling his nostrils. At some point in the past there had been an awful hiss.

He wiped the sleep from his eyes. Where was his phone? He found it on his bedside table: one voicemail message. He played it.

"Goodbye," a woman's voice said and hung up. It seemed familiar but then it sounded teary and broken up. Thomas had received messages like this in the past but never before had it ached him to hear like it did right now. The calling number wasn't listed. He wondered precisely who this girl was, what foolish thing he had done, if he would ever see her again.

"Stupid, Tom," he muttered, getting to his feet. "You're turning into a bloody slut."

He needed to get outside. He needed to breathe, walk the streets, see if a clear head could come from the experience. He grabbed his keys from the glass bowl by the door, his wallet too. Some loose change spilled out, clinking together. He shivered but couldn't place why.

* * *

Thomas roamed his neighbourhood for a little while and then beyond it. He followed a long stretch of road to the outskirts of town. This walk seemed second nature and yet, the further along he got, the cloudier his thoughts became.

He felt worst at a place called Odfellow Lane. Here his thoughts filled with shrill laughter and the awful tingling anticipation of a slap. He could only stand at the corner of the lane and stare down at the blocks of apartments ahead. For a moment, he thought of two dark-haired women, of beauty and insufficiency. He thought of sudden iridescence and severe disappointment.

"Goodbye," the woman had said.

Thomas nodded, as if he finally understood. Still the black rumble in his head persisted. Soon enough, he turned back the way he came. He could already tell that he wouldn't ever be back this way again.

OWEN TOWNEND

Owen Townend is a Yorkshire-born, Yorkshire-bred writer who is strong in the arm but only due to excessive typing. Once he has cleared the truly terrible puns from his head, he writes short speculative fiction, some of which has been published in books like *Liberty Tales* by Arachne Press, *Circling the County* by the Huddersfield Authors' Circle and The Dinesh Allirajah Prize for Short Fiction 2020 - *AI Stories* by Comma Press.

Owen did his book-learnin' at Sheffield Hallam University and now humbly claims the title of Master Bachelor of All Arts, whatever that even means. In recent years, he's become an avid collector of writing group memberships within the Yorkshire area. He is currently working on his first Western novella but the Stetson keeps getting in the way of his keyboard.

How to find Owen.
    Blog – https://mrpondersome.blogspot.com/
    Or follow him on Social Media.

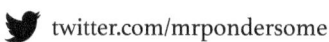 twitter.com/mrpondersome

ABOUT TIME

"TIME IS RUNNING OUT. BUT WHAT IF IT
COULD BE STRETCHED?"

TIM TAYLOR

Darkness is seeping round the edges of my vision. It takes all my strength now to keep it at bay. Just as the world I inhabit has shrunk to these four walls, what I see is being squeezed into an ever tighter space. But I can still see my daughter, red-eyed and moist cheeked, but still somehow smiling, and talking in a trembling voice about whatever comes into her head: anything but me, now, this. I don't say much in reply, but I don't have to. She talks as if her words are a lifeline and she cannot lose me as long as they are there.

"... do you remember Jason, Dad? Richard's youngest. Tall lad, blond hair. Always in trouble at school. Set himself up as a carpenter..."

I try to think who this Jason is, to put a face to the name, but I am so tired, clinging to consciousness by my fingernails. I can only raise the vaguest wraith of memory, but it will have to do. I nod.

"... well, he's been living with this girl for three years – Rebecca, she's called, Becca for short, works at the pharmacy – and they've finally decided to get married. The wedding's in March next..."

I can't hold back the dark any more. It closes in, creeping over her face and now covering everything. But there are holes in the blackness: stars and a moon. Air is rushing over my face – I'm swooping on long feathered wings, down to an ocean, silver striped by moonlight. Then, with a single beat, I soar into the sky once more.

Ahead, pyramids of deeper black blot out the stars. I ascend to fly over them, but they are too vast, too tall. Only by straining every muscle can I raise myself enough to enter the valley between them. As I do, a pale dawn light reveals them as grim rocky peaks, their bare flanks crowned by citadels of snow and ice.

I fly on, over boulder fields and mountain streams,

threadbare grass and stunted plants. The distant glow seems to be getting brighter, and mile by mile the valley descends and grows lighter, greener, wider, until I'm flying over forests and rolling hills, waterfalls and luminous blue lakes. The light ahead is brilliant now but not harsh; a warming light that floods the whole landscape with colour. A wonderful place! I want to explore every inch of it, every tree, every flower. But I am so tired, and the earth is pulling me down. There is a faint touch on my wingtip …

"Are you still with us, Dad? I was just saying, it's about time, if you ask me."

"About time for what, love? I seem to have nodded off."

"It's about time Jason got married."

"You're still talking about Jason?"

"Dad, I've only just mentioned him!"

How can that be? While I've been on my long, lonely voyage, she has spoken just a couple of words. A second passed for her, hours for me. How curious to discover, at this stage of my life, that when I close my eyes I am no longer bound to a rigid matrix of seconds, minutes, hours. So perhaps, when I leave this room for good, time will go on for me, not in some mythical place of angels, but as the infinite stretching of a single moment.

It is a beautiful thought. I don't need to fight any more. I feel my face subside into an expression it has not worn for some time. She sees it, and stops talking. A smile appears upon her face: not a brave smile but an honest one. She clasps my hand, and I tighten my fingers around hers. It is all we need to say.

The darkness is coming. But it comes in peace; I no longer fear it. A slight curl of puzzlement appears on my daughter's lips. They part as if to speak, but so slowly. As my arms become wings once more, I see that her mouth is frozen, halfway to uttering a word. And I know that she has become trapped for ever in this instant but I, at last, am free.

TIM TAYLOR

Tim (T. E.) Taylor grew up near Leek in Staffordshire and now lives in Meltham, West Yorkshire, at the opposite end of the Peak District, with his wife Rosa and 14 guitars. Having previously been a civil servant, he now divides his time between creative writing, academic research and teaching Ethics part-time at Leeds University.

Tim's first two novels: *Zeus of Ithome*, which retells the real-life struggle of the ancient Messenian People to free themselves from Sparta; and *Revolution Day*, about an ageing dictator clinging on to power, were published by Crooked Cat. His first poetry collection, *Sea Without a Shore*, was published in 2019 by Maytree Press. Tim is currently working on a science fiction project.

How to find Tim.
   Website: https://www.tetaylor.co.uk/
   Blog: https://timwordsblog.wordpress.com/
   Or follow his Social Media channels below

facebook.com/timtaylornovels
twitter.com/timetaylor1

AFTERWORD

If you enjoyed this, please check out other works by our authors and artists below and keep an eye out for other Twisted Fate titles at www.TwistedFatePublishing.com.

Thanks for Reading The Sons of Twisted Fate:

- CM Angus - author.to/CMAngus
- Gareth Clegg - author.to/garethclegg
- Nick Stead - author.to/nickstead
- Owen Townend - bit.ly/mr-pondersome
- Ian F White - author.to/Ian-F-White
- Tim Taylor - www.tetaylor.co.uk
- Aqib Ali - www.aqibaliauthor.com

And special thanks to Richard Rowan for the outstanding cover art - RichardRowanArt.com

USEFUL RESOURCES

In these uncertain times, everyone has their own periods of darkness. With that in mind, we have compiled a number of useful resources and left space for notes.

If you are struggling with any mental health problems, please check these great resources and find someone you can talk to. The old adage that a problem shared is a problem halved is true in a lot of cases and sharing your issues can make it easier to see the direction you need to travel to improve your quality of life.

Andy's Man Club — www.andysmanclub.co.uk
Andy's Man Club is a place for men to share their issues, something which has traditionally been frowned upon. You no longer need to keep your struggles to yourself. - **true male bravery is about daring to open up**, not burying your feelings away... #ITSOKAYTOTALK

.

.

.

Anxiety UK — www.anxietyuk.org.uk

Anxiety UK is a national registered charity for those affected by anxiety, stress and anxiety based depression.

Phone: 03444 775 774 (Mon to Fri, 9.30am to 5.30pm)

.

.

.

Bipolar UK — www.bipolaruk.org.uk

Bipolar UK is a national charity dedicated to empowering individuals and families affected by bipolar.

.

.

.

CALM — www.thecalmzone.net

CALM is the Campaign Against Living Miserably, for men aged 15 to 35.

Phone: 0800 58 58 58 (daily, 5pm to midnight)

.

.

.

Mental Health Foundation — www.mentalhealth.org.uk

Since 1949, the Mental Health Foundation has been the UK's leading charity for everyone's mental health.

.

.

.

Mind — www.mind.org.uk

Mind provides advice and support to empower anyone experiencing a mental health problem.

Phone: 0300 123 3393 (Mon to Fri, 9am to 6pm)

-
-
-

The Mix — www.themix.org.uk (webchat available)

Essential support for under 25s

Phone: 0808 808 4994

Crisis text message service: Text THEMIX to 85258

-
-
-

Mood Swings — www.moodswings.org.uk

Helping people recover from life's ups and downs.

Phone: 0161 832 37 36

-
-
-

No Panic — www.nopanic.org.uk

No Panic specialises in self-help recovery and our services include providing people with the skills they need to manage their condition and work towards recovery, enabling them to lead more fulfilled lives.

Phone: 0844 967 4848 (daily, 10am to 10pm).

Calls cost 5p per minute plus phone provider's Access Charge

-
-
-

OCD Action — www.ocdaction.org.uk

Information, resources and support to make a lasting difference to anyone affected by OCD.

Phone: 0845 390 6232 (Volunteer-run Mon to Fri, 9.30am - 8pm)

Calls are charged at a local rate from a standard BT land line; mobile phone charges may vary

.

.

.

OCD UK — www.ocduk.org

The national OCD charity, run by and for people with lived experience of OCD

Phone: 03332 127890 (Mon to Fri, 10am to 4:45pm)

.

.

.

PAPYRUS — www.papyrus-uk.org

PAPYRUS is the national charity dedicated to the prevention of young suicide.

Phone: 0800 068 4141 (Every day 9am to midnight)

.

.

.

Rethink Mental Illness — www.rethink.org

Rethink aims to improve the lives of people severely affected by mental illness through our network of local groups and services, expert information and successful campaigning.

.

.

.

Samaritans — www.samaritans.org

Samaritans are there day or night, for anyone who's struggling to cope, who needs someone to listen without judgement/pressure.

Phone: 116 123 (free 24-hour helpline)

-
-
-

SANE — www.sane.org.uk/support

SANE believe that no-one affected by mental illness should face crisis, distress or despair completely alone

-
-
-

Silverline — www.thesilverline.org.uk

Aimed at people over 55, The Silver Line operates the only confidential, free helpline for older people across the UK that's open 24 hours a day, seven days a week, 365 days of the year.

Phone: 0800 4 70 80 90

-
-
-

YoungMinds — www.youngminds.org.uk

UK's leading charity fighting for children and young people's mental health.

Phone: Parents' helpline 0808 802 5544 (Mon to Fri, 9.30am to 4pm)

-
-
-